# ABOUT THIS BOOK

*Welcome to the secluded mountain town of Havenwood Falls, home to sexy men, strong women, and neighbors who bite. Discover supernatural mystery, thrills, and romance in a place where everyone has a deep, dark, and often deadly secret.*

Haunted by a horrifying past, Octavia Hollows has lived her life on the move. Like all supernatural beings, when she crosses into Havenwood Falls, she sets off the town's protective wards. Unlike with most, the officials take immediate action, recognizing her as the powerful necromancer who, as a child, raised the dead in a gruesome public spectacle.

Still, they give Octavia a chance. Ninety days' probation. No dark magic. Achieve that, and she will be granted residency. They even secure employment for her at Pyntz Butcher Shoppe.

A necromancer working in a butcher shop. What could possibly go wrong?

Just when she settles in and begins opening up to the possibility of a forever home, Octavia discovers a dead body stuffed in the shop's meat freezer. He's nude. He looks like a cover model. And now, thanks to Octavia momentarily losing control of her abilities, he's alive . . . again.

Fearing someone would go so far as to kill to drive her out of Havenwood Falls, Octavia teams up with Willie, the resurrected hottie, to solve the mystery of his murder. They must work fast, though, before more corpses appear. Otherwise, Octavia could find herself booted from town along with an army of raised undead.

## HAVENWOOD FALLS BOOKS

*Forget You Not* by Kristie Cook

*Old Wounds* by Susan Burdorf

*Fate, Love & Loyalty* by E.J. Fechenda

*The Winged & the Wicked* by T.V. Hahn & Kristie Cook

*Alpha's Queen* by Lila Felix

*Ink & Fire* by R.K. Ryals

*Lose You Not* by Kristie Cook

*Tragic Ink* by Heather Hildenbrand

*Nowhere to Hide* by Belinda Boring

*Flames Among the Frost* by Amy Hale

*Rock Me Gently* by Susan Burdorf

*From the Embers* by Amy Miles

*Defying Gravity* by Kallie Ross

*Break Me Not* by Kristie Cook

*How the Dead Lie* by Stacey Rourke

*The Lurkers Within* by Danielle Bannister

*The Collector: Awakening* by Kristie Cook, R.K. Ryals, Belinda Boring & Nadirah Foxx

*Addicted to You* by Belinda Boring

*Affliction Mine* by C.J. Pinard

*The Ward & the Wanderers* by T.V. Hahn

*Toil & Trouble* by Melissa Wright

*Of Salt and Stars* by Seven Jane

*Redefined* by Morgan Wylie

*Betrayal Among the Frost* by Amy Hale

*Forever Loyal* by E.J. Fechenda

*Fate's Demand* by Emily Cyr

*The Wu & the Wand* by T.V. Hahn

*A Demon's Redemption* by JD Nelson

Also try the YA line, Havenwood Falls High; the historical paranormal line, Legends of Havenwood Falls; the darker, sexier side of town, Havenwood Falls Sin & Silk; and the local supernatural college, Sun & Moon Academy.

Stay up to date at www.HavenwoodFalls.com

# ALSO BY STACEY ROURKE

## THE GRYPHON SERIES

The Conduit

Embrace

Sacrifice

Ascension

Descent

Inferno

Revelation

## THE LEGENDS SAGA

Crane

Raven

Steam

## REEL ROMANCE

Adapted for Film

Turn Tables

## TS901 CHRONICLES

*Co-written with Tish Thawer*

TS901: Anomaly

TS901: Dominion

UNFORTUNATE SOUL CHRONICLES

Rise of the Sea Witch

Entombed in Glass

VEILED SERIES

Veiled

Vlad

# HOW THE DEAD LIE

## A HAVENWOOD FALLS NOVELLA

## STACEY ROURKE

# CHAPTER 1

"So, this is the young lady who caused the disturbance?" asked a blond woman with huge boobs and an impressive bouffant hairdo. Clicking her pen against the table top, she pursed her perfectly glossed lips, making her look even more like a middle-aged blow-up doll come to life.

"It is, Mayor." The flannel-clad sheriff looped his thumbs in the front pockets of his jeans. The tight set of his jaw gave him the look of a man so under pressure, his name should have been Bowie. "The Luna Coven was alerted by the town's wards the second she stepped into town. In her case, they mutually agreed that none of them had ever felt *anything* that even remotely resembles the energy she exudes. Fearing the presence of potent dark magic, it was decided she needed to be brought before the Court of the Sun and the Moon immediately."

Octavia's handcuffs clanked together as she raised her hand to scratch the side of her diamond stud nose piercing with her thumb nail. She was the topic of conversation, yet not one of the people seated at the table in front of her in that dank, windowless room had yet to use her name. Therefore, she purposely ignored the nameplates on the long table, refusing to acknowledge them as anything more than their superficial traits until she was acknowledged by name. With a sarcastic snort to herself, she wondered who would join the cast of characters along with newly dubbed Inflato-mayor and Bowie.

"Tell me, miss." A striking metrosexual man dragged a leisurely gaze down the length of her. He had a hint of an accent that probably made plenty of gals clutch their pearls and swoon. Octavia didn't particularly care for guys who spent more time in front of the mirror than the five minutes she did. "What are you doing in Havenwood Falls?" He was dressed in all black, like a way-too-pretty Johnny Cash impersonator.

*Huh, look who just got a new nickname*, Octavia mused to herself. *Can't say it's a pleasure to meet you, Cash.*

"Right now?" Squaring her shoulders, Octavia scanned the room with exaggerated indifference. "I'd have to say, I'm making friends and influencing people."

A severe-looking dude with an elongated face, flat nose, and frosty eyes slapped one hand on the oak table before him.

"Is this a joke to you, young lady?" the man, who would henceforth be known as Pissy Smeagol, barked.

"I found a brochure, rode into town, and *instantly* got arrested," Octavia countered, flicking her fuchsia bangs from her eyes. "So, yeah. I find that *hilarious.*"

"That's what led you here? A brochure?" A twenty-something brunette, who looked like the star of basically every teen movie ever made, chewed on her lower lip as she considered Octavia.

"Stuck right to the tire of my motorcycle," Octavia explained with an indifferent shrug that rattled the chains of her cuffs.

"If she found a brochure, she's meant to be here." Teen Movie glanced in one direction, then the other, to address the other members of the court.

"*If* being the operative word. Someone in possession of potent magic such as she is could be working for the Collector." Head listing to the side, a distinguished-looking woman with silvery-white hair hitched one brow in Octavia's direction. Octavia guessed her to be the kind of woman who always drank her tea with her pinkie finger raised for no other reason than to keep up haughty appearances. "Tell me, miss—and trust we will know if you're lying —did the Collector send you here?"

Octavia opened her mouth to deliver a snarky reply to the woman she just gave the moniker of Pinkie Finger to, only to think better of it based on the stern expressions glaring back at her. "I . . . have no clue who that is or what you're talking about."

The members of the court turned their attention to Pissy Smeagol.

"She speaks the truth." He nodded.

The members of the court seemed to let out a collective sigh of relief.

A trendy-looking grandmotherly type, dressed in a gray tunic and flowing black skirt, fiddled with the moonstone ring on her finger as her lips twisted to the side. "We all read her file. The incident at the Albany high school eight years ago is still a very concerning one."

Blinking Hip Nana's way, Octavia froze. Instantly, she sought the numb sanctuary within her as the scab was ripped off a wound from her past that refused to heal. "That . . . was an isolated incident."

"You started what was thought to be a zombie apocalypse!" a frail, elderly man with a shock of white hair grumbled. Seeing as he looked like the kind of guy who would yell at people to stay away from his trash cans, Oscar seemed the perfect name for him, in honor of that infamous grouch.

Closing her eyes, Octavia filled her lungs with a calming breath.

For a moment, she let her thoughts turn inward to find her peace in the moment. *Here, I am safe. I am powerful, rooted, and strong. Nothing is hurting me, and I've caused pain to no one.*

Expelling air through pursed lips, she opened her eyes and met the accusation head on. "I was a kid coming into powers I didn't understand. Having been bounced from foster home to foster home, there was no one to explain to me the changes I was going through. For the most part, it scared the hell out of people when they saw what I could do. Bringing the family cat back to life. Reviving grandma at her wake. Once people have said their goodbyes and let go, they find a sudden resurrection . . . jarring. And that's me putting it very, *very* mildly. They called me a devil, witch, demon, monster, and any other word you can think of that means the worst kind of evil imaginable. That led to me getting bounced around even more. Then, by some mercy of fate, I was taken in by a compassionate coven. They didn't understand my abilities, but were at least willing to offer me kindness and support. For a brief moment in time, I had a home, friends, and school. I was happier than I had ever been. Like all good things, it was a fleeting utopia that got chased away when a kid with a gun stormed the halls of North Star High . . . my high school."

The room fell silent. All fidgeting stilled.

Fighting back a hot rush of tears, Octavia cast her stare to the scuffed-up toes of her dusty motorcycle boots. "Why he spared me, I can't say. Maybe it was as simple as him not seeing me huddled and pissing myself behind the filing cabinet. Eight others weren't as lucky." Wiping away a rogue tear that streaked down her cheek, Octavia cleared her throat to steady her wavering voice. "I was only fourteen, seeing a degree of hatred and senseless violence my young mind couldn't fathom. Still can't, if I'm being honest. Cowered in that corner, armed with my abilities, I had to do *something*. In that horrible moment, it seemed I was the only one who could."

"You're a necromancer," Pissy Smeagol rasped.

"That's the technical name for it." Octavia sniffed, using the momentary diversion to get her emotions in check. "However, my talents are . . . different. Traditional necromancers can only bring people back to life for a short amount of time, and that dim spark of life makes them little more than meat puppets. I . . . can actually restore life. Back to the real deal Holyfield. I brought each of those kids back, because I thought it was the right thing to do. At that time, I had no way to know that the circumstances people die in greatly influence how they reanimate. Those kids died scared and angry, and came back consumed by enraged panic. Covered in their own blood and gore, they chased down their killer and tore him to pieces with their hands . . . and teeth. Maybe they would have stopped there. Maybe that one kill would have been enough to sate them." Octavia's handcuffs clinked together as she shrugged. "I'll never know. I can take away life that I have restored with an incantation, and raced after them in hopes of doing just that. But the cops got to them before I did. When they stumbled onto that grisly scene, they screamed the Z word for all to hear and opened fire. I had to watch those kids get gunned down a second time . . . because of me."

Teen Movie's face crumpled with sympathy. "That's horrible. I am so sorry. No one should have to endure such a thing. No one."

"On that, we agree." Wetting her lips, Octavia shifted her weight from one foot to the other.

Pressing her enormous rack against the table, Inflato-mayor spoke in a tone that was all business. "While I agree that your history is a tragic one, it doesn't address our current dilemma. We are a town built on protecting the safety and anonymity of our supernatural and human residents alike. And you have a very public paranormal scandal in your past. Were you witnessed using your powers? How did word get out of what had happened?"

5

"One student saw me." Behind her eyes, Octavia could still see the color drain from that pudgy-faced boy's skin the moment he saw the first of the fallen students twitch with life. His frantic screams as he ran away would forever echo through her mind as the soundtrack of guilt that was hers alone to bear. "He told anyone that would listen. No one believed him. Except for the tabloids, of course. I got write-ups next to possible alien abductions and Bigfoot sightings. He made me an urban legend, of sorts, and got himself committed for his efforts. For a while, at least. Last I heard, he was getting out. I truly hope that's true."

Again, they all looked to Pissy Smeagol, who paused before bestowing his wise nod.

Hip Nana with the moonstone ring squared her shoulders and peered Octavia's way directly. "The talents you possess border on the brink of the dark arts, Miss—" her gaze flicked down at the file spilling Octavia's secrets for all to see—"Hollows."

Octavia longed to be past the point of explaining herself to people. Sadly, it was a reality that followed her everywhere. Well, almost everywhere. For a while she had found acceptance in the most pure and loving way. A love, the kind sonnets were written for and ballads were dedicated to, once swelled her heart and made happily ever after seem within reach. Tragically, even *that* had been stolen from her.

"I'm of the mindset that no one and nothing is born bad or dark. This is who I am. It's a part of me, whether I like it or not. It's not evil. It's biology."

Rubbing his palm over the stubble of his chin, Sheriff Bowie narrowed his eyes in Octavia's direction. "Since then, you've been living as a drifter, and found your way to Havenwood Falls?"

"Honestly?" Octavia tugged at the bottom hem of her dingy T-shirt. It was due for a wash, as was she. "In the flyer, it looked like a nice place. That's basically the extent of the forethought that went into my decision to come here. But that's what I do. I go somewhere new, find some odd jobs to get by, and stay until I've worn out my welcome."

"What a lackluster existence," Oscar grunted, tapping his cane against the floor.

Octavia filled her lungs and exhaled her tainted truth. "Yes, it is. People learn what I can do and suddenly they either want me to wake grandpa up and find out where he buried his money, or they chase me from town with torches and pitchforks. With the reception I've gotten here, I will say this seems like more of an *option two* kind of town."

"You won't have that problem here." Cash chuckled. "We have enough undead folks walking around here anyway."

"Need I remind you," Inflato-mayor interjected, "the fact that she found the town at all is proof she is *supposed* to be here."

"How do we know she's not going to visit the nearest cemetery and raise an army of corpses against us?" Oscar snipped.

"Come on!" Teen Movie shoved her chair back from the table and turned to face Oscar head on. "How do we know the vampires won't drain all the humans dry? How do we know the witches won't turn everyone into frogs? How do we know the wolf shifters won't hump everyone's legs? Havenwood Falls is a city based on a civility to all kinds! It's one of our town's founding principles. We deny her that, and we are denying the acceptance and respect this town was founded on."

Face folding into a mask of distaste, Pissy Smeagol laced his hands and set them on the tabletop. "Apparently, we're revealing *all* of the town's secrets today."

Despite the somber situation, a half smile tugged at the corners of Octavia's lips. "I put the pieces together before that, thanks. You all came to terms with the whole necromancer thing shockingly quick. Plus, I get the faint traces of a vampire in the room. The dead call to me. It's a thing. No offense to whoever that refers to."

"None taken," Teen Movie muttered with a half grin. "Mostly because I only came close to dying, never fully committed to it."

"FYI, I can make your heart beat for a few minutes if that's something you're ever interested in." Octavia casually lobbed back the offer.

"Are you hitting on me?" the pretty brunette asked, fighting back a laugh.

Octavia's head fell to her shoulder as she tsked in disappointment. "No, but I wish I was. That would be a hell of a line."

"It really is," Teen Movie chuckled, eyes crinkling with amusement. "But since my heart is still beating, it's sadly wasted on me."

"Enough!" Pinkie Finger drummed her fingernails on the table in exasperation. "We simply need some sort of assurance that you aren't going to raise the dead while you're here."

Octavia's mouth fell open, yet for a moment words failed her. Her truth gave her pause. Every time she spoke it out loud, it left a fresh scorch or scar on her already battered heart. Swallowing hard, she forced out the facts as life had dealt them. "One hundred and eighty-three days ago, the man I love died. If I was going to bring anyone back, it would have been him."

Crossing his ankle over his opposite knee, Cash broke the heavy hush that followed. "I have a rather fun idea. Sheriff Kasun, does Pyntz Butcher Shoppe still have a help wanted sign in the window?"

"Of course!" Oscar snorted, shoulders shaking with laughter. "No one wants to work for Guy! No one would step foot in that grumpy old coot's shop if it weren't for his prices."

Sheriff Bowie—as Octavia would continue to think of him until he bothered to utter her name—puffed his chest and considered Cash with narrowed eyes. "It is. But you couldn't possibly mean . . . ? I mean, that's cruel even by your standards."

Leaning back in his seat, a wicked smile coiled across Cash's lips. "Seems to me that would be the very best place possible to test her."

Pinkie Finger responded with a curt nod. "I'll reach out to Guy at once and offer to double my sponsorship for his annual Chili Cook-Off if he allows her to fill the position. Now then, did you have accommodations lined up, miss?"

Steeling her spine, Octavia met her glare head on.

To her surprise, Teen Movie piped up on her behalf. "*Octavia.* Her name is Octavia, Saundra. Since we bled all her secrets out onto these polished wood floors, the least we can do is offer her the dignity of addressing her by name. And yes. She does have a place to stay. I have a room for her at the Whisper Falls Inn that she can use for as long as she needs."

Casting a glance down at the nameplate on the table, Octavia acknowledged her new ally with a face full of gratitude. "Thank you, Miss Petran. But I don't take charity. I'll take you up on the offer, and pay my way with money or hard work."

Teen Movie—no, *Michaela*—offered her a winning smile. "Sounds like we have ourselves a deal. Do you have a car here? You can follow me over there when the meeting is done."

Raising her cuffed hands, Octavia pushed her bright pink bangs behind her ear and tried unsuccessfully to stifle a laugh. "No, I . . . uh . . . actually drove a motorcycle here. Into the mountains . . . where cold was invented."

"Bless your heart, Octavia!" Hip Nana—Mathilde Augustine according to her nameplate—adjusted the collar of her tunic that had shifted to one side. "I swear, we should hand out winter coats and gloves the second someone crosses the town line."

"Just motivated me to ride all that much faster," Octavia

admitted, dropping her hands in front of her with the clink of metal.

Sheriff Bowie said nothing, but cleared his throat in disapproval.

Swiveling her chin his way, Octavia feigned innocence. "Come on, let's not build our relationship on a bed of lies. In the scheme of things, me speeding is, like, a best-case-scenario offense."

Unable to help himself, the sheriff's head fell back as he let out a bark of laughter. "Octavia, I have a sneaking suspicion you're about to cause me miles of paperwork."

Leaning his way, Octavia bumped his elbow with hers and read the name on his badge. "But think of the stories you'll have to tell, Sheriff Kasun."

Folding her hands on the table in front of her, Pinkie Finger tipped her head back to allow her the perfect angle to peer down her nose in disdain. "If we are done with the chitchat, I propose to the Court that we grant Miss Hollows a three-month probationary period in Havenwood Falls. During her time here, she will stay at the Whisper Falls Inn, and maintain employment at Pyntz Butcher Shoppe."

Oscar's nostrils flared as if smelling something that disgusted him. "A necromancer in a butcher shop? I, for one, wouldn't eat anything her tainted hands have touched."

"I beg you to stop," Michaela muttered out of the corner of her mouth.

If Pinkie Finger heard him, she didn't let on, choosing instead to continue on with her duties. "This is the motion I am putting before the Court, although I do wish Addie was here to record all of this."

Clearing her throat, Mathilde's expression turned sour. "She's handling imperative matters pertaining to the other, far more crucial, crisis at hand."

Putting her hands beside her mouth, Octavia whispered in the tone of someone genuinely trying to help, "I'm new here, but I think she means that Collector person."

Pinkie Finger silenced her with a glare. "Yes, quite. Now, who holds proxy for our absent Court members?"

Inflato-mayor raised her pen in the air. "Lilith Blackstone."

"Odette Alverson," Cash added, with the lift of a finger.

"The terms have been stated. As such," Pinkie Finger, known to the rest of Havenwood Falls as Saundra Beaumont, continued, "if her probation ends without incident, she will then be welcomed into the town. I cast my vote in favor."

"There is some petty shit going down here, and I'm here for it." Cash—Roman Bishop as he would be known if he ever bothered to acknowledge Octavia as a person—cast his vote with the lift of one expertly manicured hand. "I second her terms."

"I think it's safe to fault on the side of discretion," Oscar—aka Lawrence Mills—grumbled, and rapped his knuckles on the table. "This plan has my vote."

"If the town wants her here, it will reveal to us why. I vote in favor." Pissy Smeagol—known to others as Elmsed Fairchild—dipped his chin to his chest in support of the ruling.

Dragging her fingers through her mahogany locks, Michaela shook her head. "I guess, since you already have your majority vote, it doesn't matter that I think this is cruel and unjust considering her magical attributes?"

"Looks like a verdict for erring on the side of discretion." Even as he spoke, the sheriff unlocked Octavia's handcuffs and set her free.

Grabbing her gavel, Mayor Barbie—reading that name on the plate nearly made Octavia snort at the irony—held it at the ready. "The motion passes." One bang of that gavel sealed Octavia's fate. "You are allowed entry to Havenwood Falls, Miss Hollows, but make no mistake as to our intentions. The Blackstone witch hunters are all around, so there will be no hiding any usage of the dark arts. At the very first sign that you've committed an offense against your probation, you will be cast from the town and the wards strengthened to ensure you never step foot over town lines again."

"Thank you for the opportunity," Octavia muttered, swallowing down the acidic burn of regret scorching up the back of her throat. "I will do my best not to let you down."

This was far from the warmest welcome she had ever received entering a new town, but also far from the harshest. At least this time didn't involve a lynch mob . . . yet.

# CHAPTER 2

*W*ith her Scrambler parked at the curb, Octavia sat on a bench with one leg tucked under her. Killing time until her meeting with someone named Addie from the Luna Coven, she occupied herself by envisioning this Addie person to be a round-faced old lady with an excess of crystals strung around her neck and reeking of patchouli oil.

Fighting against the chilled breeze lashing her hair into a bird's nest, Octavia shoved on a Detroit Tigers hat she had picked up a few towns back and fed her ponytail through the back size-adjusting loop. While the russet-colored bomber jacket she wore would have been no match for the fall chill on its own, partnered with a flannel shirt and hoodie, she was comfortable enough to enjoy the scenery and people watching. That could be counted as one of the handful of benefits to not having more than a backpack full of belongings. Another being that it never took her long to decide what to wear.

Chewing on her cuticle, Octavia scanned the landscape. A water fountain, carved with leaping mermaids, sat in the center of the town square, bubbling a soft serenade to the townsfolk ambling by. Quaint businesses lined the streets, each lovingly maintained and cozily inviting. Swelling behind the picturesque town was a majestic mountain range that cradled it like the setting of a precious jewel. Nice as it all was, Octavia couldn't grant herself any more than a passing interest.

Admittedly, it was a cute town. No one could deny that.

Still, she had been in some of the very cutest, and numerous others that could only be classified as armpit real estate. In the long run, it didn't matter. Like so many locales before this, her stay here would be temporary. Life had taught her the lesson time and again that she wasn't allowed roots.

"I think that's the necromancer," a voice whispered behind her.

Octavia turned to see two teenage girls strolling past. The shopping bags they carried read *Callie's Consignments*. The taller of the two, who had been the one to point Octavia out to her friend, tossed a curtain of golden locks over her shoulder.

The other, with a pixie cut styled into a faux-hawk and impossibly long lashes, scrunched her pert face in confusion. "What's wrong with neck romancing? I saw you do that with Kurt after Friday night's football game. You didn't seem to have a problem with it then."

Chin falling to her chest, Octavia pressed her lips into a tight line and tried—unsuccessfully—to stifle a laugh.

Stupefied by her friend's response, the blonde stopped and blinked in her direction. "Not neck romancing, *necromancing*. Bringing things back from the dead."

"Ooohhhh. You know we shouldn't be talking about things like that! Kurt would be uber pissed if you got your family booted from town all because you have a big mouth."

Octavia didn't think it was her imagination that sudden judgment and contempt crept into the teen's tone. Whether it was directed at Octavia or her friend, she couldn't be certain.

Prior experience in such matters still made her hackles raise defensively.

"Hey!" Blondie called out, causing Octavia's hands to clench into fists at her sides.

Chin jutting out in rebellious defiance, Octavia forced herself to turn a mask of indifference their way. "Yeah?"

The blonde met her stare not with contempt, but a warm smile. "Tonight's the last night of the season for Saturday Movies in the Park. The whole town will be there, giving summer an official send-off with a National Lampoon marathon. Some of John Hughes's finest. You should totally come. It's in the big park, and everyone brings blankets or chairs. It's a big thing. It would be a great way for you to meet people and get to know the town."

"O-okay." Octavia frowned, mystified by this strange and unusual development. *What the hell was this place?*

"By the way, rumor has it you're a regular badass. Welcome to Havenwood Falls!" An elbow to her friend, and the blonde resumed her sassy stride.

Momentarily unable to form words, Octavia watched them fade into the distance. Only when they had shrank to little more than specks did she finally utter, "That . . . was not the reaction I usually get."

"Well, Havenwood Falls isn't like other places," a female voice interjected, edging alongside Octavia. "Hey, Octavia. I'm Addie. Did you get settled into the inn okay?"

Pushing off the bench, Octavia rose to her feet. The young woman staring back at her was nothing like what she pictured. Actually, she looked like a less emo Avril Lavigne. Like, to borrow a metaphor from the song, he was a boy, and she was a girl, and she took great pleasure in making things *anything* but obvious. If nothing else, Octavia was happy to see someone else with a nose ring in what she had begun to fear was a vanilla town. "I dropped off my backpack and grabbed a room key. That's as close to settled as I get."

"We'll see about that." Addie snorted a knowing huff of laughter and strode past her toward the businesses lining one side of the square. "We've got a lot to do. Let's start by introducing you to your new boss."

Falling into step beside her guide, Octavia scanned the line of storefronts for their destination. She found its red brick nestled into the middle of the row. The ornate iron door was painted black, yet scuffed with white to give it a warm, worn feel. The wide display window was emblazoned with the company's logo. Octavia couldn't hold back a laugh as she read that along with the tag line. "Pyntz Butcher Shoppe: Meet Your Meat. That's great. Marketing at its finest. Really, it should be the slogan for Grindr."

"What's that? A butcher shop from another town?" Addie tipped her face in interest, brown eyes blinking Octavia's way.

Wetting her lips, Octavia opted for the conversation of least resistance. "Yes. Yes, it is."

"I'm totally fucking with you. I know what it is. This isn't Mayberry, Octavia." Pausing at the curb, Addie waved to the driver of a burgundy pickup truck as he puttered past. With a jerk of her head, she led Octavia across the street.

Squinting at the window display, Octavia tried to make out the smudged yellow lettering beneath the shop logo, which appeared to have been painted on in a rough freehand. "What does it say under the tag line?"

Rolling her eyes, Addie shook her head. "It says 'Your mama liked my hot dog size.' There was a tiny incident last year at a town event that *some* people just can't seem to let go of."

Octavia would have found the humor in that, if it wasn't for the pull of death luring her toward the shop. Tempting . . . urging . . . calling her to the unthinkable. Chewing on her lower lip, she swallowed hard and tried to remember why she was subjecting herself to this. She could hop on her bike and ride until the air wasn't cold enough to hurt her face.

"Is Mr. Pyntz nervous about having me here? Is that why you're chaperoning our meet and greet?"

Curling her hand around the doorknob, Addie pulled the door open and set off a chime from within.

"Goddess be, no! Guy is a cranky asshat. I'm here to make sure he doesn't chase you out with a meat cleaver." Holding the door open, she invited Octavia in with a formal wave of her arm and a beaming smile. "After you."

"How could I resist such a warm welcome?" Stifling a groan, Octavia jogged up the three brick stairs into the store.

Despite the taunting roar of death screaming at her from all sides, it seemed like a nice place. One glass and chrome display case ran down the right side of the shop. A giant chalkboard on the brick wall behind that was etched with the menu prices and daily specials. The soles of her motorcycle boots scuffing across the walnut-stained wood floor, Octavia inched her way up to the counter. Peeking over, she locked eyes with a man no more than four feet tall. Wisps of brown hair covered his otherwise bald scalp, and a deep scowl cut deep divots between his bushy brows. Peeking out from under the rolled sleeves of his red flannel shirt were forearms thick from years of wielding a cleaver. Locking his glower with her wide-eyed stare, he brought his blade down hard and fast, slicing a rack of ribs in two.

Shoving her hands into the pockets of her jeans, Addie approached the counter without an ounce of hesitation. "Guy, this is Octavia, your new helper." Leaning Octavia's way, Addie whispered for her ears alone, "He's a hobgoblin. They aren't known for having great people skills. Hardest workers you'll ever meet, though."

Another whack of his cleaver served as his only response.

"Are you going to play nice?" Addie asked, hitching one brow, challenging him to argue. "Or do I need to alert the Court of your refusal of *their ruling?*"

Gruff expression sagging in annoyed defeat, Guy brought his cleaver down for another slice.

Leaning in Addie's direction, Octavia muttered out of the corner of her mouth, "Does he talk?"

Clapping her hand on Octavia's shoulder, Addie offered her a comforting squeeze. "He does, but it's often *really* unpleasant. He has been known to make customers cry using only his words."

Another hack, this time with a bit more sass behind it.

Instead of releasing her hold on Octavia, Addie guided her toward the waist-high swinging door that led behind the counter. "Guy, I have to tattoo her. Can we use your office?"

A snort and a nod were the closest the butcher had come to actual conversation up to that point.

Wanting to slam on the brakes, but knowing the terms of her probation wouldn't allow it, Octavia reluctantly stumbled along. "I'm sorry, what now? There are a few key points of that sentence I need a tad more info on."

Letting the half-door swing shut behind them, Addie took a sharp left to lead Octavia into the office. The cramped space overflowed with boxes of receipts and shipping orders, and the three filing cabinets that lined the back wall exploded with long-forgotten paperwork that had never been properly filed. With a sweep of her arm, Addie cleared off Guy's desk. Her lips screwed to the side as she watched the cascade of papers flutter to the floor. "Anywhere else, I might almost feel bad about doing that. Here, I feel like I actually helped."

Leaving Octavia's questions floating in the air, Addie busied herself pulling her tattoo gun and ink from her handbag.

"*Tattoo?*" Octavia finally formed her question, feeling it was a crucial topic to address. Preferably *before* any needle touched her skin. Sure, she had numerous piercings—both above and below the belt—but she had yet to etch her skin with ink. Something about the permanence of that made her commitment-phobe nature break out in hives. "No one mentioned permanently embedding ink in my skin. I for sure would have remembered that."

"Well, it's not exactly permanent—at least until you become a resident—but it's standard protocol for those with supernatural abilities that are allowed to visit Havenwood Falls. It binds everyone to the wards of the town. In return, everyone gets a little benefit for themselves. For example, vampires are granted the added bonus of being able to walk in the sun." Taking a seat at Guy's desk, Addie leaned back to plug her gun into the outlet. "You should see them when they try out *that* talent for the first time. Ever see Carlton's dance on *The Fresh Prince of Bel-Air*? It's like that, but with significantly more spinning."

Grabbing a folding chair from the corner, Octavia slid it across the floor and took a seat opposite Addie. "Are there other ways you can enchant it? Maybe to dull my powers? Because, honestly, I'm petrified I'm going to bring the display of whole chickens alive in some grisly headless fowl kick line that—while maintaining stellar choreography—will still scare away Guy's customers, and get me booted out of town."

Loading the gun with black ink, Addie paused and blinked in Octavia's direction. "Sure, absolutely." One shoulder rose and fell in a noncommittal shrug, her tone far from convincing. "I'll subdue your powers to a spark instead of a jolt. How's that sound?"

"That would be amazing." So desperate was she for that level of relief, Octavia was willing to ignore Addie's apparent lack of certainty.

Picking up on the necromancer's urgency, Addie dragged her

tongue over her bottom lip and cautiously explained, "The Court won't allow you a permanent mark. Not yet, at least. This one will last the length of your stay here. If you're granted residence, I can extend it."

*Almost one of them, but not quite.*

Octavia was familiar with the cut of that feeling. Its message had been sliced into her at every foster home the system kicked her into.

"Totally understandable," she muttered with a tight smile.

"Wow, you have just the worst poker face ever," Addie said with a humorless laugh. "It's three months, Octavia. Three little months. Then I can enchant the ink to a permanent status without another needle prick. All I need to know now is what design you want."

Octavia filled her lungs, allowing herself a brief moment of contemplation. In an instant, the design chose itself. "The mascot of my school back in Albany was the Navigators. I want the navigational star of a compass." Tucking a loose strand of hair that had fallen in her eyes back under her hat, Octavia tried to belittle the emotional impact of the moment with a smirk. "Maybe it will finally help me find my way."

Gun prepped, Addie rested it on its pedestal and dug her alcohol wipes and image transfer papers from her bag. "That's a beautiful sentiment, and I think it's already working. How else do you explain finding yourself in our hidden little town?"

Octavia turned her hand over and offered the artist her wrist. "I don't think it was fate that brought me here as much as a piece of garbage."

After free-handing a design onto transfer paper, Addie held it up for Octavia's approval. Eyebrows rocketing into her hairline, Octavia gave an enthusiastic nod at the beautiful piece of artwork. Wasting no time, Addie situated the paper on Octavia's offered arm.

Biting the inside of her cheek as she concentrated, Addie

pressed the transfer paper into place. "No one ends up here by accident. Maybe I can help fill in some blanks for you with a few more details to this story?"

"A brochure for the town blew across the street and stuck to my leg. Not exactly kismet," Octavia muttered, bracing herself for the bite of the needle.

Flipping a switch, Addie fired the gun to life and filled the room with its reverberating buzz. "There has to be more to it than that. That's just part of the magic of this mystical little burg. She knows when people need her. So, set the scene for me. Where were you? How did it happen?"

Octavia bristled at the first touch of the needle. Inhaling through her nose, she exhaled through pursed lips. "I had been working at a consignment shop just outside of Chicago. Things went south—in an incident with a mousetrap I don't care to repeat —and I was skipping town. I was astride my fiancé, Elba's, motorcycle. His sister gave it to me after he died. Anyway, I was idling at a red light when a brochure from Havenwood Falls tumbled out into the road and stuck to my leg. I had nowhere else to go, and the people on the brochure looked so . . . happy. It seemed like a great idea, right up until your sheriff slapped on the cuffs."

"You were sitting on the bike of the man you loved?" Addie echoed, carefully outlining the design.

"Uh . . . yeah." As the needle twanged over a tendon, Octavia grimaced.

As she made it to the edge of the compass, Addie's brow furrowed with concentration. "Seems to me you had a spirit guiding you here, which wouldn't be a far-fetched notion. Spirits have a stronger presence here than they do in the land of the magically deficient. Maybe Elba steered you here. It wouldn't be unheard of for him to be bonded to that motorcycle in some way, if it was important to him. Maybe he has an agenda all his own, and it required you to be here."

"No!" Octavia snapped, with more force than necessary. Clearing her throat, she fought to soften her tone, despite the venom of bitterness seeping through her thought process. "Elba is dead. He's gone. I can't . . . let myself entertain *any* other options."

Her art work complete, Addie sprayed the fresh tattoo with water and swabbed it clean. Covering it with a sterile pad, she taped it into place. "Slow your roll. I was just suggesting a theory. I will say, if there is even a small part of you that wants to make Havenwood Falls your home, you need to open yourself up to this place and the people. You may find an acceptance here no other town can offer."

After unceremoniously collecting her things, Addie gave Octavia a supportive bump to the shoulder and exited the shop with the tinkling chime of the bell.

Left alone with her new boss, Octavia cradled her freshly tattooed arm to her chest and ventured back out into the front of the store. Her mouth opened and closed, searching for some way to engage the cranky shopkeeper, only to be halted by his pointed glower snapping in her direction.

"You marked?" he pressed, bringing his cleaver down on a fresh T-bone.

"Yeah," Octavia confirmed, holding up her bandaged wrist.

Dipping his head in approval, he glared at the door as the bell chimed once again. "I'll handle slicing the meat. You juggle the customers."

"Because you're worried I'll bring your inventory to life?" Defeat crept into her voice, forced there by her own conviction that she would fail at this impossible job.

Pulling back as if she'd slapped him, Guy's pug nose crinkled, the look making him seem more bat than man. "No. Because I hate people and don't want to talk to them." Another chime of the door interrupted their awkward exchange. "Go see what they need."

Wetting her arid lips, Octavia approached the counter to find a painfully attractive couple practically dry humping in front of the display case.

"Can I help you?" Octavia asked through a cringe. "Or offer you a prophylactic?"

The guy, all strapping muscles and good hair, nibbled on the neck of his sweetheart.

Giggling, the buxom blonde with him swatted playfully at his arm wrapped firmly around her waist. "Can we get two tenderloins please? Cut extra thick."

"She's a girth snob," her amorous boyfriend chuckled, nuzzling into the crook of her neck.

"You're so bad!" The blonde giggled.

Repressing the urge to heave, Octavia pivoted on the ball of her foot to find Guy staring her way with gleeful amusement.

"Two *thick* tenderloins," she parroted.

Slapping the cuts onto butcher paper, Guy balanced them on the scale. "A pound and a half, at $11.98 a pound."

He peered her way expectantly as she shuffled to the register and hen-pecked at the keys.

"Your total is . . . 17.97." Accepting their payment, Octavia handed over the cuts of meat to the pair that had since diverted their attention by slobbering all over each other.

Only after the bell chimed, and the shop door swung shut behind them, did Octavia hold up her index finger in protest. "Okay . . . *ew.*"

"Newly mated shifters," Guy offered in place of explanation. "They have no self-control."

"So that's just something you get used to living here?" Octavia shook off a chill of disgust.

"No," Guy countered, his mouth twisting into a wicked smile. "I cut them extra fatty slices, hoping it will give them the runs and ruin the mood."

"You're diabolical." Octavia's expression fell slack as she blinked his way with newfound respect. "Adopt me and teach me your ways."

Granting her a snort of laughter, Guy returned to his slicing.

With the tingling warmth of momentary acceptance coursing through her, Octavia let herself believe for a split second that coming here hadn't been a colossal mistake.

A slew of towns, a plethora of people; one was sure to stick.

Right?

# CHAPTER 3

TWO AND A HALF MONTHS LATER . . .

*I*f Octavia were to describe the magic of Havenwood Falls after her sixty-plus days living there, she could think of no better term than an afghan of comfort knitted around all of its visitors and residents. In her brief time there, she already felt more settled than she had in a long while. Not that she was ready to plant roots quite yet. Let's not get crazy. Still, she was finding it fun to try on how the other half lived, like playing a role in a production of *Normalcy: The Bliss of the Mundane.*

Bounding down the stairs of the inn, she hummed a Nirvana song under her breath that had been stuck there since karaoke night at the Haven Saloon two days ago. Rounding the corner, she pulled up short to avoid slamming into Michaela, who had an armload of freshly folded towels.

"Morning, sunshine." Michaela beamed. "Need fresh towels in your room?"

"I'm good for another day." Skirting around her, Octavia

plucked an orange from the fruit bowl on the counter. Tossing it in the air, she spun around and caught it behind her back. "Although you are going to need to bleach the ones up there now. They did not fare well against my freshly colored hair."

Rolling her eyes, Michaela chuckled. "I thought it looked particularly blinding today. Hey, are you opening at Pyntz?"

"Sure am! I'm even flying solo until two. Guy said he needed a mental health break until then. I think it's to recover from his BOGO sale yesterday. He had to interact with too many people. His body is recovering from having to be nice." Curling one shoulder in coquettishly, Octavia wiggled her eyebrows. "Why? Did you want me to bring you back an afternoon latte from Coffee Haven?"

Hugging the towels to her chest, Michaela expelled a breathy sigh of appreciation. "That would be the kind of angelic act that would make me forgive pink-stained towels."

Cracking open the skin of the orange with her thumbnail, Octavia strode for the door with laughter bubbling from her lips. "As you have requested, so shall it be! See you at two twenty with caffeine in hand."

Bundled in the heavy winter coat the Colorado winter made her buy, Octavia munched on the citrus slices as she strolled through town with the keys to the shop jangling in her pocket. She waved to Callie unlocking her consignment shop, and glanced in the window at her latest stylish display. The aroma of the day's fresh-baked pastries wafted from Coffee Haven, filling Octavia's head with longing for the blueberry scone she would treat herself to at the end of her shift. Much like every day Octavia worked, Madame Tahini was peering her way from the threshold of her storefront, Madame Tahini's Potions, Lotions, Palm Readings, and Other Extra-Sensory Services. On more than one occasion she had begged Octavia to let her do a reading on her, but Octavia feared that particular can of worms contained a python. Best to leave the lid firmly in place.

As of late, it seemed the Court had stepped up their security detail. Members as well as the police made themselves seen much more often, prowling the town at all hours of the day and night— always watching, always on alert. The details of why remained cloaked in mystery. Octavia felt on occasion that they seemed to be watching her more closely than others, but wrote it off as paranoia.

At the front door of the butcher shop, Octavia took a beat to finish the last of her orange. Wiping her sticky fingers off on the legs of her pants, she dug out her keys and hurried inside to escape the cold. Shrugging out of her coat, she rounded the counter for the back room with Nirvana still playing on an endless loop in her mind.

"*What else should I say? All apologiiiiiiiies,*" she sang to herself, not caring in the least if those were the right words or not.

In the middle of Guy's desk, she found a note written by the antisocial hobgoblin himself. Plucking it from the clutter, she read aloud, "Everything that needs cutting is cut. Stay the hell away from my knives. CDI delivered a shipment last night. If it's slow, check the inventory against the shipping invoice. Remember, a member of the Court is supposed to stop by for a spot inspection. Keep the place standing, and don't fuck anything up." Wadding up the note, she tossed it in the trash. "He missed his calling. A man capable of such heartfelt sentiments should be writing for Hallmark."

After finishing off the morning prep, she turned the sign to *Open* and unlocked the door. Of course, there was no instantaneous rush. The vampires didn't come until later in the day, due to habit more than necessity, and humans normally didn't start thinking about meat options until around lunchtime. The wolves were normally the shop's first customers. They would start wandering in around ten, in between patrols. Out of busy work, Octavia grabbed the shipping invoice from the envelope on the back desk and sauntered to the walk-in freezer.

"*Wish I felt like you, easily amuuuuused,*" Octavia sang. Hand closing around the door knob, she pulled it open to the hiss of escaping icy air. Gaze fixed on the list, she was scanning for where to start when a solid mass of cold meat slammed into her. The force knocked her off balance. Unable to catch herself, she crashed to the ground with the weighty lump on top of her.

Skull bouncing off the floor with a *thunk*, Octavia's vision blurred, her elbows barking with pain from the impact. Blinking hard to focus, she was oblivious to the tendrils of green crackling from her fingertips until her vision sharpened on a pair of lifeless gray eyes boring into her. She was pinned under a body. A dead one. This frantic realization came a heartbeat too late, literally. Her biology took over before she could even hope to suppress it. A crackling emerald wave coursed through the corpse.

A spastic shudder.

A deathly rattle.

Then, those gray eyes blinked once . . . and again.

Shoving her way out from under the rousing corpse, Octavia curled into a defensive crouch with her eyes bulging in their sockets.

"No, no, *no!*" she screamed through clenched teeth. In her mind, she watched the possibility of life in Havenwood Falls float away on the breeze of a grisly misunderstanding. "This can't be happening. It isn't . . . *isn't* happening. No! I refuse! I refuse to acknowledge this as my truth."

Sucking down gulps of air like a man surfacing from the depths, the corpse stumbled to his feet. Silver eyes—a side effect of the reanimation magic—blinked in search of answers.

He was scared.

He was confused.

He was . . . very, *very* naked.

Holding up one hand to shield herself from his dangling participle, Octavia tried to turn into the spin of this spiraling situation. "Hey there . . . Mr. Man. You're probably a little freaked at the moment, which I totally feel ya on. But do you remember anything at all? Like how you ended up dead and naked in a walk-in freezer?"

"C-c-cold," the humansicle stammered, his blue lips quaking.

"Here." Untying her apron, she tossed it to him. "It's not much, but it'll cover the parts that need covering. What's your name?"

Octavia risked a glance his way through her fingers, and instantly regretted it. Not that he was gross. Far from it, actually. Flaxen hair fell across his forehead. The rippling muscles of his physique were toned and taut as he stumbled in a small circle in search of answers. He was sexy in a Frankenstein's monster kind of way. It was admitting *that* to herself that made Octavia judge herself horribly.

"I . . . I don't know," he croaked, tying the apron around his waist with trembling hands.

Gratefully dropping her arm, Octavia peered his way with her pulse hammering in her temples. "Okay, well we have to call you something. How about . . . Willie?" Instantly, her face blanched. "Oh, God. Because I found you in the freezer and thought of that little penguin cartoon. Not because I saw your thing. But . . . I totally saw your thing. Sorry."

"Willie," he tried the name on, sampling its feel on his tongue.

"Any idea how you died, Willie?" Even as she asked, her gaze searched him for clues of his demise. He had no ghastly bullet holes. No stab wounds that were evident. Other than a scar on the right side of his abdomen, a few inches from his belly button, his gray-tinged flesh was unmarred.

"I . . . died?" he managed, in a rebuttal Octavia was in no way prepared for.

"*Fuck.* Yeah, a little bit. But you're back now. So, *yay!*" Even Octavia heard the lack of conviction in her tone. "Speaking of, how are you feeling? Any uncontrollable rage or aggression bubbling beneath the surface that I should know about?"

"No." A brief shake of his head, and Willie peered her way as if noticing her for the first time. "But how? How am I . . . back?"

"*Yeeaah,*" she drawled in her uncertainty. "I may have had a little something to do with that."

"You're . . . magic?" he stammered, hunting for clarity.

Stalling for time by rubbing her palm back and forth over the back of her neck, Octavia searched for the right words. "The technical word is necromancer. It basically means you didn't have a pulse, and now you do. You're welcome."

*Yeah, there was probably a smoother way to say that.*

Shuffling a step closer, Willie raised his hand as if to brush her cheek, only to have her shrink away from his touch. "If that's true, the power you hold must be an immeasurable one. How is that possible? You look like an ordinary girl. Albeit one that had an orange for breakfast. You have a sliver of rind on your chin." A brush of his knuckle knocked away the lingering remnants of her snack.

Jerking at the chill of his touch, Octavia slapped his hand away. "You know what I wish? That dead people would stay dead, or at the very least, keep their damned hands to themselves!"

The ding of the front door froze Octavia on the spot. Grabbing Willie by the wrists, she yanked him down beside her on the floor close enough to feel the chill off his clammy skin.

"You're sending really mixed messages," Willie pointed out, only to be hushed by her finger to his lips.

"Get back in the freezer. *Now*," Octavia demanded in an urgent whisper that left little room for debate.

She fully expected him to argue, as anyone sans pants would when asked to walk into a room that would shrink their outtie into an innie. To her surprise, he responded with a resolute nod and waddled in a crouch into the icebox from which he came.

Bouncing to her feet, Octavia kicked the door shut behind him. A quick beat to smooth her rumpled clothing, and she rounded the corner into the showroom with a fake smile plastered in place.

That grin died on her lips when she saw who was waiting at the counter with his hands plunged into the pockets of his designer suit coat.

"Balls . . ." Catching her expletive mid-utterance, Octavia dove to save her slip-up. "Shhhip, Roman *Bishop*. What brings you in today, sir?"

Not the smoothest cover up, but having a Court member there at *that* particular moment killed Octavia's last little bit of cool.

One corner of his mouth tugging back, he tilted his head and considered her through narrowed eyes. "This is a butcher shop. What I'm after seems pretty straightforward."

Jaw swinging slack, Octavia tried to wrap her mind around what the hell was happening. "*Meat!*" she blurted after a beat, jamming a thumb in the direction of the writing on the window. "You're here to *meet your meat*."

"Among other things." Roman winced at her manic display. "I detected a surge of magic, and here I find you, twitchy and sweating profusely."

"I'm fine!" Realizing she was talking a few octaves too loud, Octavia cleared her throat and tried to remember what her normal voice sounded like. "Just moving around slabs of—" once again she pointed to the sign—"*meat*."

*For the love of God, stop using visual aids.* She mentally berated herself.

"Your enthusiasm for your job is . . . impressive." Something in the way he uttered that last word made it sound less than complimentary.

"What can I say? I love—" *Don't you dare say meat*—"my job."

"An admirable trait. However, it still doesn't explain the crackle of energy I felt." Eyebrows raising to his hairline, Roman challenged her to deny what he knew to be fact.

With the warning that any magic would be felt within the wards resonating through her mind, Octavia opted to turn into the spin of a spiraling situation. Slumping against the display, she filled her lungs to capacity and rambled out her explanation in a long-winded rant. "It's being around all this . . . death. It's *so* much harder than I ever thought it would be. I can't relax, can't drop my guard for even a second. When I do, my control wavers. I've gotten tired a couple times, and there were . . . slip-ups." Seeing the vicious gleam in Roman's stare at her admitted failure, Octavia hurried to add on the necessary disclaimer. "But don't worry! Each time lasted no more than a fraction of a second, and I undid the effects before anyone could see anything!"

For a beat Roman merely stared, eyeing Octavia like a bug that should be squashed under his foot. "I see," he finally managed, his mouth opening with a crisp pop. "You realize, of course, I will need you to recreate the act to confirm that was the magical charge I felt."

"Recreate . . ." Trailing off, she peered down at the sliced tenderloin as if rescue could be found there.

"Should be quite simple for someone with talents of your caliber." The heels of his expensive wing-tip shoes clapping over the wood-planked floor, Roman strode to the door. "I'll lock this to ensure no customers stroll in, and you'll grant me proof I can take to the Court."

"Yeah, absolutely," Octavia chirped. Smile stuck in place, her brain screamed the expletive-filled tirade she could not.

Lifting his fingers in a bored fashion, Roman used magic to click the lock, then returned to the counter with his arms folded across his chest in anticipation of her performance.

Knowing the T-bones to be the freshest in the case, Octavia slid down the counter to them. Breathing in deep, she plugged into the vat of energy simmering within her core. Hand beside her thigh, she snapped her fingers once, twice, and again. The third strike released a spark of green from between her fingers. Energy primed and ready, she roiled it from one fingertip to the next with slow waves of her digits. Emerald wisps danced over her skin, casting a haunting glow over the whitewashed brick walls. Lowering her hand, she made gentle contact with the cold slab of meat nearest her. A twitch. A tremor. Then a pulse thumped through the tissue as if still attached to a live cow.

Despite his stern façade, Roman's mouth fell open as he took a step closer. "Remarkable."

As she flattened her palm to the palpitating meat, Octavia's emerald tendrils vanished. Dropping her chin to her chest, she closed her eyes. "Spirit from beyond the grave, I brought thee into light. With your help, I cannot stave. Return thee into night."

Life faded from the tissue, and the meat stilled.

"Easy ritual on a hunk of flesh. Harder—and more wrought with guilt—on a living, breathing person," Octavia muttered, more to herself than her audience of one.

Eyes narrowing in her direction, Roman considered the odd, pink-haired girl as if seeing her for the first time. "That . . . was quite impressive. Not to mention it perfectly matching the surge I felt before."

Heart pounding against her ribs, Octavia fought to keep her expression a casual neutral. "So, that's it then? Spot inspection passed?"

"Not entirely," Roman scoffed with an arrogant smirk. "You have yet to take my order."

"*Oh, shit!*" Octavia blushed, giving herself a quick forehead smack with the heel of her hand. "Sorry, what can I get for you?"

Adjusting the collar of his black tweed coat, he jerked his chin toward the case. "I'll take two of those T-bones, including the one you manipulated. I'm quite curious as to what twice-dead beef tastes like."

"I touched it without a glove." Octavia cringed, then rolled her eyes at that ludicrous proclamation. *Because* that's *the problem with Lazarused meat—germs.*

"I think I'll be okay," Roman huffed with a wry laugh as Octavia shoved on a pair of gloves. Despite an obvious distaste for small talk—made blatantly clear through his sideways glances, sneers, and repeated checks of his watch—he begrudgingly played the part of polite patron and attempted the bothersome task. "So, is everything going well for you here? You're enjoying Havenwood Falls?"

In that instant, Octavia found her calm—in the truth. Laying the steaks down on the white paper, she eased them to the scale to get their weight. "I really am. After being different and feared my entire life, this is the first time I've ever felt *seen.* Seen for more than my freakish abilities."

Lips pressed into a firm line, Roman nodded in feigned understanding. "Yes, quite."

Printing off the price sticker, Octavia affixed it to the neatly folded and taped package. "Which is why I want to do everything I can to prove myself to the Court. I hope that's what you'll tell them when you report back about this little visit."

Accepting his order, Roman tossed two twenties across the counter. "It will indeed. For *today*. Bear in mind, however, that a lot can happen in what remains of your probationary period, and we *will* be watching."

Without waiting for his change, he turned on his heel and strode out to the tune of that jingling bell.

Expelling a breath she hadn't realized she was holding, Octavia darted to the door. Pausing a beat to make sure Roman didn't turn around for any reason, she locked the door behind him. Flipping the sign to *Closed*, she sprinted back to the walk-in freezer.

The door creaked open, chilled air puffing out in roiling clouds. Tentatively inching inside, Octavia scanned the space with a wary gaze. All she found were frozen hunks of meat.

"Willie?" she ventured, all the while saying a silent prayer that she had imagined the entire encounter. Hallucinations she could deal with; reanimated corpses were another matter.

Nothing but stifling silence answered.

"Yoo-hoo," she tried again, in a sing-song voice. "Previously dead guy I really hope I imagined . . . ?"

Nothing.

Shoulders sagging with relief, Octavia closed her eyes and said a silent prayer of thanks to the heavens.

"Is he gone?" Willie asked, his head popping out from between two hanging slabs of beef.

Screaming in surprise, Octavia stumbled back. Green sparks sizzled from her fingers as she fell onto a whole pig that came in with the latest order.

With a shudder, the pig squealed to life. Wriggling out from under her, it bolted out of the freezer in a flurry of flapping ears and clapping hooves.

Octavia could only stare after it, damning her horrible luck. "Son. Of. A. Bitch."

# CHAPTER 4

*A*fter cornering the squealing pig in Guy's office, Octavia scooped him under her arm in a football hold. Thankfully, he was no bigger than a bull terrier, which made pork transport relatively easy. The little porker announced his protest in a shrill screech sure to make the ears of any werewolves in a five-mile radius twitch.

Quietly shushing him, Octavia gave him a comforting scratch under the chin. She toyed with the idea of uttering the spell to rescind her magic from him, but couldn't bring herself to do it. How could she give him piggy snuggles one second, and sell him for a roast the next?

"Shh, you're okay. It's alright." Glancing up to Willie she whisper-shouted, *"How the hell do you calm down bacon?"*

Willie raised his hands, palms up, gesturing for her cargo. Out of ideas, she handed him over. Sure enough, by the time Octavia opened the freezer door—the only place she could think of to keep her mess hidden for the moment—her little pink companion had settled into contented snorts.

Only then did Octavia realize Willie had zipped himself into a pair of jeans somewhere along the way. "Way to holster your weapon, soldier."

Easing the piglet to the floor, he peered up at her from under his brow. "Whoever stuffed me in here either left *my* clothes behind, or *theirs*. Either way, I'm taking advantage."

"What?" Forehead creasing, Octavia peered around for other clues or oddities. "They hung you up like a pressed suit and left your knickers folded behind you? Who does that? That's, like, some weird mafia shit. Did you find a horse head in your bed recently? Get the kiss of death from a guy with a horrible fake accent?" Bending down, she gave the pig a pat to the head as he wandered past.

"That . . . I don't know. But while you were chasing the piglet past the display case and apologizing for his fallen brethren, I was looking for something a bit more concealing to put on. I found a satchel in the corner by the whole chickens." His chin jerked toward the back of the freezer. "There was no wallet or identification. I'd say this was robbery gone wrong, if I hadn't been frozen . . . and nude."

"*Maybe*," Octavia's head listed to the side, floating an idea, "they brought you in here and did weird sex stuff to you. Do you think that could be it?"

Arms falling slack at his sides, Willie cringed. "Well, I do *now*!"

"Sorry." Kicking the door shut behind her, Octavia prevented the pig from darting out a second time. "Was there anything else in the satchel? Clues to who you were before the mansicle?"

Willie scooped the bag up from beside him, his head disappearing into the suede fabric. Unfortunately, that gave Octavia a prime view of his sculpted abs. Swallowing hard, she directed her focus to the piggy instead. His curly little tail and wriggling little snout were both adorable and a welcome distraction from the hot undead guy.

Finishing his cursory inspection, he reappeared with a hooded Henley sweater and a frown. "Nothing in there but the disappointing realization that I may have been *really* preppy."

Glancing over her shoulder toward the storefront, Octavia nervously chewed on her lip. "Okay, so you've got clothes, and you aren't dead anymore. I think both of those fall in the win column, and bring our time together to a close. There's a shuttle that runs out of town throughout the day. You're good to grab the next one straight out of here. You can probably find the schedule at the Chamber of Commerce. I don't have much money." Digging into her back pocket, she pulled out a twenty-dollar bill and a gum wrapper. "But eating every day just makes us greedy, right? So, you take this, hop a bus out of town, and . . . yeah . . . this has been great."

Ducking into the gray Henley, Willie tugged it over his head.

"I can't leave," he countered, combing his fingers through his hair. "Someone tried to kill—no, someone *did* kill me. Whoever it is, they're still out there. They figure out it didn't stick, and they'll find a more *permanent* alternative. Like dynamite, or dropping an anvil on my head."

Crouching down to scratch the pig in one of its random paces past, Octavia stifled what was sure to be a manic peal of laughter. "In these death scenarios, are you exclusively Wile E. Coyote? Or do you take the form of various Looney Tunes characters? Because, really, I think the likelihood of either of those things ever happening falls into the category of slim to none."

"But the *threat* is real! That's what I'm saying," he exclaimed, waving an arm at what had been his freezer tomb. "And it's not exclusive to me. Someone shoved a dead guy into the path of a— what did you call it? Oh, a necromancer! Yeah, seems to me, someone was setting you up."

Cold realization crept in with a chill that rivaled that of the freezer. "A Court member showed up right after I brought you back. You're right. Someone *wanted* me to get caught. But who? And why?"

Looping his thumbs in his front pockets, Willie chewed on his lower lip. "If that was their intention, they aren't going to stop at one failed attempt. For all you know, there are more bodies to come. Our only option, to keep me alive and you free of an unintentional army of undead, is to find who's behind this and expose them."

Melting to the floor with a groan, Octavia let her head fall back against the frigid metal wall. "So, somehow this has turned into a buddy-cop caper? No one hates their life more than me right now." Hooves clicked across the floor in scurried steps. Nosing at her hair, the pig sniffed at Octavia's face. Head lolling to the side, she went nose to snout with him and gave him a scratch behind the ears. "I've decided to call him Bacon. My other choice was Spam, but I feel it makes his origins seem questionable."

"Octavia?" Edging closer, Willie ducked his head, trying to catch her eye. "You get that we have to figure this out, right? It's a matter of life and the absence of death."

"Potato potahto," Octavia said with a humorless laugh. Almost as an afterthought, she peered up at him with a questioning frown. "Hey, how did you know my name? Not quite sure we had reached that point in our relationship."

"Maybe something magical passed between us. *Or . . .* maybe I read your name tag." Willie tapped his own chest to remind her where her own name tag was pinned. "Now that we solved that mystery, can you at least *acknowledge* the more detrimental situation at hand?"

"Nobody likes a snarky ex-corpse," Octavia grumbled under her breath. Bum good and icy, she shoved herself off the floor. "So, someone is trying to make sure I don't stay in Havenwood Falls, huh? Then, it's official. I can no longer count on two hands the number of towns I've been chased from."

"Could be worse. I could have been assaulted by a necrophiliac." The moment the words left his lips, Willie convulsed in a full-body shiver. "Nope, too soon to joke about it."

"You're new to this, let me catch you up." Octavia rubbed her hands together to warm them up. "This is the point where I have to decide if it's worth it to stay and try to make it work, or hop on my bike and make that physically and emotionally frigid ride to Gonesville."

Pallor slowly transitioning from ashen to a golden beige, Willie folded his arms over his chest. "What's it going to be?"

Chewing on the inside of her cheek, Octavia's nostrils flared. "This town has great coffee, damn it. And the people don't treat me like a freak. I *won't* be bullied into leaving. Not this time. If *Scooby-Doo*-style shenanigans are required to stop the asshat behind this, that's exactly what we're going to do. Whoever stuffed you in here had to get you in somehow. *That* means there's a good chance they will be on the security camera footage. Bring the pig, Willie. We've got a murder to solve."

# CHAPTER 5

"*E*njoy your ribeye." Fake smile plastered in place, Octavia handed Rusty—a local shifter—his order. "It's so fresh it'll taste like you chased it down yourself. Only, you know, you won't end up with hair caught in your teeth. Shit, that's not offensive is it? I'm talking a lot, aren't I? Can we just pretend I said have a nice day and move on with our lives?"

Pausing at the door, Rusty's only response was to hold up his order and nod.

"Yep, handled that beautifully," Octavia grumbled under her breath. Peeling off her gloves, she tossed them in the trash. "Not awkward at all."

Ideally, she would keep the butcher shop closed and go into hiding until the whole living-dead debacle was worked out. Unfortunately, in this tight-knit town, someone would definitely alert Guy if she dared keep the shop closed. That was a surefire way to rile him up into a Pyntz-sized fit. Not to mention how incredibly suspicious that would look to the members of the Court.

Taking advantage of the lull between customers, she darted back to the office with the soles of her Chuck Taylors squeaking across the floor. Willie was waiting for her in Guy's office. With Bacon nestled snug in his lap, he rubbed the soft skin of the sleeping pig's ear back and forth between two fingers.

"Do you think he remembers how he died?" Willie asked when her shadow filled the doorway. "If I can't, maybe he doesn't either."

"I've seen video footage of slaughterhouses. If he doesn't remember his trip there, that is a *very* good thing." Nose crinkling at the memory, Octavia strode to the filing cabinet in the corner, where an old ten-inch analog TV was hooked to possibly the last working VCR in existence. "This is some high-tech security Guy has in place here."

Hitting the eject button, she waited through three minutes of whirring and clicking before the geriatric VCR spat out the video.

"Is that even going to work? If he repeatedly records over the same tape, it'll be distorted . . . if it plays at all." Brows pinched tight, Willie posed his next question to the wall. "How do I know that? As a millennial, I shouldn't possess this information. Unless . . . oh, God. *Was I a hipster?*"

"Okay, first, Guy changes the tape every day when he comes in. This one is dated yesterday. It should be the one." With the pads of her thumbs, Octavia pushed the tape back into the hesitantly receptive machine. "As to your brewing identity crisis, there wasn't a beanie cap in that bag, or a pair of stupidly small glasses, so I think you're in the clear."

The cassette settled in, the control buttons illuminating. Turning the knob, Octavia clicked on the TV to a screen of white static. Index finger hovering over the play button, she swallowed down a lump of unease lodged in her throat. Somewhere on that tape was a person capable of murder, and hungry to get rid of her.

Easing Bacon to the floor—where he turned in three circles and lay down with a huff—Willie joined her in front of the television. While his flesh had warmed, it still lingered a few noticeable degrees away from the norm. "Just because we find out who it is doesn't mean we have to go after them ourselves. We can go to the police, show them what we found."

"That would have been an option if I found a dead man in the fridge, *and the story stopped there.* No dead guy, no crime. Thanks to me, and this wonderful little curse of mine, we're on our own." Octavia pressed play, crackling the video to life. The camera was positioned at an angle in the hall to capture the freezer door and the display counter, specifically to protect Guy's inventory. In the lower right-hand corner of the screen, a clock counted off the time. "I was here until eight last night. It had to be after that."

Hitting the fast-forward, she thrust the mind-numbingly dull activities of butcher-shop life into overdrive. Slowing at eight o'clock, she watched time tick by with nothing more than sliced meats and tuna steaks to show for it.

Vision beginning to blur from the grainy feed, Octavia was rubbing her eyes with the heels of her palms when Willie's hand seized her wrist. "What is *that?*"

Eyes popping open, Octavia scurried to press play and slow down the feed.

Leaning in, the pair squinted at the grainy footage, trying to decipher what was happening. The shop was dark. The timestamp of 11:37 was a clear indicator the shop had long since closed for the night. In the hallway, just out of camera range, something jerked in and out of view.

"Is that . . . flannel?" Face scrunched up, Octavia tilted her head at different angles, as if they would somehow provide a better vantage point.

"I think so." Reaching out, Willie pointed to one spot in the bottom corner of the screen. "And that looks like hair."

"So what we have here is someone trying to drag something heavy through the hall." Rocking back on her heels, Octavia scanned Willie's frame. "You're not a huge dude, but I bet as dead weight it would take some effort to maneuver you around. Do you want to—"

"No, we're not going to try it." Cutting off her budding idea, Willie's stare never left the TV. "Wait! Pause it!"

The person on the screen took a step back, giving a full view of his flannel shirt and wisps of thinning hair. Hunched over, hands curled around the edge of what looked like a tarp, the mystery form moved it with determined tugs and scoots. Pausing, he stood to stretch his back . . . and cast a cautious glance up at the camera.

Octavia's index finger tapped pause, freezing the image in place.

She sucked in a shocked gasp, her heart hammering against her ribs. "That's . . . *Guy*."

"We know Guy?" Willie muttered out of the corner of his mouth.

"His name is on the front door. This is *his* shop."

"Oh." Hesitantly, he pointed at the screen. "He . . . uh . . . he's dragging something heavy on a tarp."

"I'm aware of that." She forced the words through clenched teeth. She had spent every day with the cranky little hobgoblin. She had even come to find his ways endearing. How was it possible to be *that* wrong about someone?

Face folding in concern, Willie cast a sideways glance in her direction. "How well do you know this Guy?"

A click, and the tape cut off, awakening the crackle of static.

"What happened? Is it over?" Octavia reached for the eject button, her hand pausing when a warbled voice seeped from the television.

"*Ruh ih.*"

Glancing to Willie over her shoulder, she found his stupefied expression matched her own. "Did you hear that?"

"I did, but really wish I hadn't—"

"Shhh, shh!" She cut him off, frantic hands slapping him quiet.

"*Rummm diiiiiieeee.*"

Palms up, Willie shook his head. "Drinking and driving campaign?"

Leaning in, ear inches from the screen, Octavia held up a finger to hush him.

From within the snow of static, a face swelled, stretching out from the screen like a beast crawling its way out of the pits of hell.

Clamping her lips down on the scream lodged in her throat, Octavia fell back into Willie. Her fingernails scraping his skin, the two clung to each other as another deathly rattle bellowed from the apparition.

"*Ruuuuu . . . guuuuuy.*"

Convinced she had heard the word *run*, Octavia needed no further prodding to comply. Spinning and sliding in her mad scramble, she snatched Bacon off the floor and sprinted from the office with Willie hot on her heels.

# CHAPTER 6

*P*acing from one side of her room at the Whisper Falls Inn to the other with her phone to her ear, Octavia twisted her hair around her index finger and rambled into her Bluetooth. "I'm really sorry, Guy. I just had to get out of the shop before I contaminated all the meat and customers. Stomach flu. Hardcore. Stuff firing out of both ends."

Sprawled on the bed, scratching Bacon's belly, Willie winced at her colorful wording.

She plucked the earpiece from her ear as the sounds of Guy's rant filled the room.

"Yes, I locked up," she interjected when he paused for a breath. "And I didn't puke anywhere weird . . . that I remember." Reconsidering the state she left the shop in, she tacked on for good measure, "But, just in case, you should probably stay out of your office until I get a chance to clean and sanitize basically everything in it."

Cue second round of heated hollering.

Eyes closed, Octavia nodded along, with her lips pressed in a thin line. "Yes, I will be there tomorrow, as long as the symptoms stop. Really, what's happening in my colon can only be described as fiery and explosive . . . Hello?" Lips drooping in a downward C, Octavia swiveled her stare to Willie. "He hung up on me. I gotta say, it took longer than I thought it would to get him to that point."

"You would have lost me at your chorus of pantomimed dry heaves. Those were both convincing and disturbing. Listening to that was almost as hard as sneaking Bacon in here." At the mention of his name, Bacon rolled off Willie's lap and trotted to a bowl of popcorn they had snagged from the vending machine for him.

"Well, I'm not exactly crazy about the idea of having either of you here, but renting a second room for the night isn't exactly within my budget." Leaning against the dresser/ TV stand, Octavia crossed her feet at the ankles and shoved her hands into the pockets of her Tennessee Titans hoodie.

"Hey." Scooting to the edge of the mattress, Willie reached out and caught her pinkie finger with his. "I would never hurt you. I hope you know that. You *literally* gave me a second chance at life. You're my miracle, Octavia. My angel. Words cannot express how grateful I am for you."

"S'no big deal." Staring down at his hand cradling hers, a rush of guilt reddened Octavia's cheeks. She couldn't deny she was attracted to him. Blond hair fell across his forehead in stylish disarray, his silver eyes peering at her with an intensity that took her breath away. Not since Elba had anyone looked at her like that. Much as she hated herself for thinking it, he made being undead look *good*. "I just wish you remembered, like, anything from your past. Maybe then we could find some intertwining parts of our lives that could help us figure out why anyone would target the two of us."

Playfully tugging at her hand, Willie offered her a charming smile that caused a deep dimple to dip in his right cheek. "You could tell me about yourself. Maybe it could spur some memories of my own? Where'd you grow up? What brought you to Havenwood Falls? Do you have some big burly boyfriend who's going to come breaking the door down for me being here? See how I cleverly worked in the question to see if you were single? Pretty suave for a former corpse, huh?"

"The suavest." Shaking her head with a laugh, she pulled her hand away and mashed it back into her hoodie pocket. "But we're not going to play Twenty Questions with Octavia Hollows right now."

"Octavia Hollows, a name almost as pretty as you."

She halted his roll with the raise of one finger. "Pump the brakes, cowboy. You can slather on the charm all you want, but you're still sleeping on the floor tonight."

Shoulders sagging, Willie looked at her like she was the only star in an otherwise black sky. "It's not a play toward anything. I just want to get to know you."

The simple idea of opening up about her sordid past caused Octavia to bristle. Pushing off the dresser, she grabbed the coat they had smuggled Bacon in under and tossed it to Willie. "Maybe later. Right now, someone needs to take Bacon out for a walk before this place starts to smell like a petting zoo."

"I have no problem waiting." Willie grinned, shaking out the coat for a round of pig-wrestling. "Thanks to you, now I've got all the time in the world."

Hiding a coy smile behind her hand, Octavia watched him cradle Bacon under the coat and disappear into the hall with a wink. The moment the door clicked shut, she settled onto the bed, hands gripping the comforter in tight fists. She bit her lower lip as a chill rocked through her, causing a rash of goose bumps to crawl down her arms. She thought it was a rush from a bit of harmless flirting . . . until her breath left her lips in a frosty white puff.

Movement at the foot of the bed snapped her head around.

There, a shimmering form stared back at her. Throwing herself back, she scrambled up the mattress and climbed the headboard. A shriek escaped her parted lips as the figure floated closer, one transparent hand reaching for her. Eyes bulging, Octavia's heart locked in a vise grip of anguish. The apparition—she recognized it.

"*Elba?*" His body was little more than a wafting shadow, but the shape of his face and soulful eyes was forever written on her heart.

Chin to his transparent chest, the words left his blue lips in a haunting tremor. "*Wroooong guy.*"

Two words were all it took to morph Octavia's blind terror into livid frustration. "Are you freakin' kidding me? You come back from the great beyond to play the part of jealous boyfriend? All this time my heart has been broken, aching for you, and *this* is what it takes to bring you back?"

"Wrooooong guuuuuuy." His ethereal form flickering, Elba slowly faded from sight.

"Yeah?" Octavia flopped down on the mattress, feeling the loss of him all over again, this time ground in deep with a dull blade. "But at least he's *here.*"

With a ripple, Elba was gone.

## CHAPTER 7

"You sure you want to go in to work today?" Stretched out on the bed, Willie leaned over the edge of the mattress to tickle Bacon's snout, an effort that earned a merry snort of appreciation. "You could hang out with Bacon and me, and *not* be in the presence of a possible murderer. Sidebar question—are we really sold on the name Bacon? What about Repig? Because he pigged, but now thanks to you, he gets to pig again."

Tying her hair up in a messy bun, Octavia blinked hard at her reflection in the bathroom mirror, hoping a little refocusing was all it would take to make her look less like a worn-out crack addict. It didn't work. A sleepless night in a room with the undead will do that to a person. Whatever this twisted arrangement was, it needed to be short-lived.

"Yes, I really do have to go in to work. If Guy is behind this, we need to find a little bit more substantial info to go on. Also, the pig answers to Bacon. We change it now, and we're just going to confuse him."

Throwing open the bathroom door, Octavia strode across the

room to collect her coat and wallet. Stretched out on the bed, his denim-clad legs crossed at the ankle, Willie tracked her every movement with silver eyes.

Feeling heat travel up her neck to her ear lobes, Octavia tried to remember what her normal, not in any way aroused, voice sounded like. "Ahem, so . . . yeah. Don't forget to take Bacon for walks. But stay close. Your eyes are seriously right out of a sci-fi movie. Anyone who sees them is going to know you're some kind of freak, and the last thing we need is people asking questions."

Rolling onto his back, Willie tucked both arms behind his head and wiggled his eyebrows suggestively. "Yet another reason to stay; I really *am* some kind of freak."

Realizing he was lying on her gloves, Octavia smacked at his leg until he reluctantly moved it. "Who are you kidding? Any freak tendencies you may have had, you can't remember. For all you know, you were into being diapered."

Biting his lower lip, he playfully nudged her hip with the side of his foot. "You wanna diaper me?"

Freezing, Octavia could only blink in his direction for a minute. "Really? Do you feel comfortable with that line? You sure that's the one you want to go with?"

Lips twisting to the side, Willie dropped his arms to his sides and pushed himself onto his elbows. "When you get home from work, can we pretend that didn't happen?"

Grabbing her gloves, she strode toward the door, if for no other reason than to hide her smile. "I think that would be best."

"WHERE'S MY PIG? And I don't mean the purple plate painting kind!" Guy hollered the second the door to the butcher shop door dinged open, announcing Octavia's arrival. Handing over a whole chicken to a customer, Guy impatiently waved to the next in line. "You, what do you want?"

"Pork loin?" The redheaded customer asked, suddenly unsure of her choice to enter the hostile shop at all.

Nodding with a snort, he hopped down from his footstool to fetch it. "CDI dropped off our order the other night. On the truck they had a little suckling pig no bigger than a cocker spaniel. I can't sell that!"

"Cocker spaniel?" Rounding the counter, Octavia tied on her apron. "Not bull terrier?"

"Call it whatever kind of mini-canine you want, I can't sell it!" Pausing mid-rant, Guy's beady eyes narrowed in her direction. "Are you still contagious?"

"Nope! Slept off the funk." Plucking disposable gloves from the box on the counter, she wriggled her hands into them. "So what's with the piggy that came to market?"

"It's gone! Did they come to get it? I told them I wanted that sorry excuse of a pig gone!" Jumping back up on his stool, he barked at the customer, "17.59."

Flinching at his harsh tone, the customer threw a twenty at him, collected her order and dashed for the door without bothering to wait for her change.

"Yes." Face vacant of emotion, Octavia saw an opportunity and went for it. "That's exactly what happened. They came . . . and took the pig back."

Arms crossed over his chest, he glared up at her, lower jaw jutting out in annoyance. "Where's my refund? I checked the register twice. It's not there."

"It . . . wasn't in the register," she repeated, buying herself time to think. "And how much was that refund again?"

"Seventy-two dollars."

"Seventy-two!" Octavia squeaked in a high-pitched tone that

would make wolf shifters cringe. "Wow. No, yeah. They totally gave that to me. But . . . it was in between my frantic trips to the bathroom. So I shoved it in the pocket of my apron to give to you today."

Rolling his shoulders, Guy looped his thumbs in his pockets. "Which you'll be doing now?"

"I will, of course." Octavia nodded, chewing on the inside of her cheek. Mentally, she tried to account for every penny presently in her possession. "Uh . . . little heads up, some of the refund came in the form of Canadian coins and a rewards card for a free pizza."

Rolling his eyes, Guy jerked his head toward the office as another customer entered the shop. "I never get your humor. Money on my desk. *Now.*"

Emptying her pockets, Octavia dumped out every dollar, penny, or lint fuzzy onto Guy's desk. Only after turning her wallet upside down and shaking out its contents was she able to come up with enough to officially buy herself an undead pig.

Begrudgingly coming to terms with the fact that eating was a luxury she wouldn't be enjoying for a couple days, Octavia was stuffing her wallet back into her back pocket when a file poking out of the desk drawer caught her attention. Shooting a quick glance to the door to make sure Guy was nowhere in sight, she quietly plucked the file from its resting place.

Her blood ran cold to see her own name scrolled across the tab. When she flipped the file open, every newspaper article written about her debacle in Maine slipped out, some fluttering to the floor. Guy had been researching her past. Had he deemed what he found adequate reason to get rid of her by any means necessary?

# CHAPTER 8

*B*undled in winter coats and practically every item of clothing Octavia owned, she and Willie hunkered down behind a row of bushes in the town square, peeking through the branches toward the butcher shop. The cloak of night draped over the town, yet it still gleamed with a midday glow thanks to the elaborate holiday decorations. Glancing around, Octavia could see a cornucopia of customs represented in the splendid display. Nativity scenes were set alongside yule pentacle wreaths. Menorahs sat on windowsills next to beautifully lit Christmas trees. Lovely as it was, Octavia would have appreciated it more if she wasn't stalking a potential killer.

"The cold has now reached my brain. I may forget my name a second time." Willie shivered. "Remind me again why we're doing this?"

"Guy was on the security tape, *and* he has a file on me in his desk." Feet prickling from the cold, Octavia shifted her weight from one foot to the other to try to get the sluggish blood flowing through her lower extremities. "The second he leaves the shop, we're going to follow him and see what we can find out."

Peering at their mode of transportation waiting at the curb, Willie's mouth opened with a pop. "We're going to follow him on your *motorcycle*, when it's like fifteen degrees outside? We're not worried about drawing attention to ourselves, or, you know, sliding on the ice and crashing to our doom?"

"If someone *does* notice us, it may result in us having some much needed backup when we burst in on a possible homicide. I, for one, would not turn that down." Even as she uttered the words, Octavia leaned closer to Willie in search of the added body heat.

"What about the crashing to our doom part?" he countered.

"If it's your skull that gets cracked against the pavement? Well, then you'll be damned lucky you're traveling with a necromancer."

"And if it's you?"

"Then we're both fucked." Seeing Guy flick off the lights and lock the door behind him, Octavia pinched the sleeve of Willie's borrowed coat and yanked him along behind her as she scooted farther down the shrubbery. "He's heading to his truck! Come on!"

Running in a crouch behind bushes strung with holly berries and white twinkling lights, they darted toward her bike. While the snow had stopped, a light dusting still remained over the leather and chrome.

"You are just the worst motivational speaker, ever. Hey, quick question: at no time since moving to the Colorado icebox did you think it might be a good idea to upgrade to something with—I don't know—*doors*?" Kicking a leg over the seat, Willie settled onto the bike. Instantaneously, he emitted a pained yelp as the cold bit right through his pants to the tender regions beneath. "My balls have now ascended so far north, they're tonsils."

"The town is small. We won't have to go far." Shoving on her helmet, Octavia passed the other to Willie. She waited for him to snap it on before propping the bike up with one foot and kicking it to life with the other. Her beloved beast woke with a rumble. "Hold on tight. Oh, and on the off chance we start to slide on the ice, don't put your foot down. That's a good way to shatter every bone."

"No part of that was comforting!" Willie yelled over the growling engine, and wrapped his arms around her waist.

Hanging back far enough to avoid being spotted, the pair trailed Guy to Blaekthorn Lumber. As he parked out front, Octavia guided the bike into a neighboring alley to wait and watch. Needing the heat of the engine, they kept it running as a temporary mercy. Octavia could feel Willie's thighs pressing against her hips. She may even have found the moment somewhat sensual—if her own snot wasn't frozen to her face.

"How long are we going to give him?" Willie asked, tone quaking from the force of his chattering teeth. "Because, if I'm being honest, the walk-in freezer was warmer than this. While we're on the topic, why does he even *have* that? He could save the electric bill and store everything outside. Sure, it might not be up to health code, but—"

"Shut up!" Octavia inched the bike forward, ready to take off the second Guy's truck moved. Seeing him reappear, her eyes widened to saucers at his chosen purchases. "Look-look-look! That's a roll of duct tape around his wrist! And it sure as hell looked like he just threw *a tarp* in the back of his truck!"

Glancing over her shoulder, she exchanged matching looks of dread with Willie.

Wetting his wind-chapped lips, Willie spoke the ominous thought running through both their minds. "Those are supplies to move a body. I think he has selected his next victim."

LAGGING A SAFE DISTANCE BEHIND, Octavia and Willie tailed Guy to his cottage-style house on the outskirts of down. Killing the engine a block away, they hid the motorcycle beneath a giant pine tree and made the rest of the trek on foot. While Guy's truck sat in the driveway, not one light had been turned on within the cottage.

Catching Octavia's arm, Willie held her back, his voice dropping to an urgent whisper. "What if he's already killed again? He could have the lights off so no one can see him move the body!"

"If we catch him in the act, this will all be over." Peeling his fingers from her arm, Octavia jerked her head for him to follow. "Come on."

Sticking to the shadows, the frozen duo squeezed themselves between the truck and row of trees lining the driveway. The detached garage lay before them, pitch black inside. They tried the knob only to find it locked up tight, without a hint of movement within.

"Where the hell did he go?" Octavia whispered, her heart pounding against her ribs.

Nudging her with his elbow, Willie nodded to a flickering light coming from the back of the house. "There's a storm cellar. A terrifying, swallowed-by-the-earth storm cellar."

Hatch-style doors were thrown open wide, beckoning them into the looming maw of the unknown.

"I think now would be a great time to call the cops." Willie emphatically nodded in support of his own idea. "I mean, they're equipped to handle this sort of thing without shrieking like little girls. Which I most certainly will do if we go in there. So—to avoid that—I say we call them, and their guns, and—"

"Shhh!" Octavia hissed. Catching Willie by the collar, she tugged him into a crouch beside her. "Being in possession of a tarp isn't illegal. We need more than that to go on. You know what that means."

"I don't want to say what that means."

"Say it."

"I don't want to."

"Speak our truth. Let it set you free."

Shoulders sagging, he groaned. "We have to go in."

"We have to go in," Octavia parroted. Clapping a comforting hand on his back, she led him in an awkward duck waddle across the backyard.

Pausing at the mouth of the hatch, they held their breath and crept down the rickety wooden stairs. A bare bulb swung overhead, cobwebs covering the cracked cement walls. Feet scuffing over the floor, they found themselves surrounded by paint cans, assorted tools, and the undeniable scent of dryer sheets.

Using the flashlight on her phone, Octavia ducked under low-hanging duct work to scan the darkness. The shimmer of light reflecting off shined metal caught her eye, drawing her attention to a metal tarp grommet. Pulling up short, her arm shot out to halt Willie.

"Look," she whispered, nodding her head in that direction. "The tarp."

Edging in tight to her side, Willie's hand protectively encircled her wrist. "We need to go. What if he's already made his kill?"

"Without proof, we've got nothing," Octavia's urgent whisper matched the intensity of his. "We both want to be safe. That starts by finding out—"

The sound of a chainsaw's growl sliced off the end of her sentence.

Scooting around behind Octavia, Willie sheep-dogged her back toward the stairs. "That's our cue to exit! Up and out! *Now!*"

Unable to formulate an argument that could counter a chainsaw, Octavia ran for the stairs. She was just one stride away from the bottom step—with the freedom of the starry night looming overhead—when Guy appeared from behind the chugging furnace. Eyes hidden behind safety goggles, he held the chainsaw poised before him.

Scrambling for distance, the trespassing duo backpedaled posthaste.

Raising her hand in front of her face, as if such a gesture could repel a chainsaw, Octavia yelped, "*Guy*! I'm sorry. We shouldn't have come. We were looking for you and saw a light on."

Letting the chainsaw's rumble speak for him, Guy held it at shoulder height and stalked forward, driving them further and further from any hope of escape.

"If it makes any difference, we didn't see anything," Octavia gushed in a long-winded ramble.

"Nothing at all!" Willie added, gaze swiveling in search of a weapon.

"There's no reason you can't . . ." The tarp crinkled under Octavia's shoe, alerting her that she'd let him guide her right to his kill room. "Oh, hell."

Tripping over the edge of the tarp, Willie went down hard, landing on his tail bone and elbows.

Guy's attention fixed on Octavia. Chest rising and falling, he inched in closer.

Her breath coming in agitated pants, Octavia inched backwards, all the while saying a silent prayer not to trip over chopped up body parts like Willie had his own feet.

"I messed up, Guy. Trespassing was intrusive and deadly. I've made a horrible mistake, and I see that now." Voice morphing to a plaintive plea, Octavia felt a wafting chill skitter up her spine. She was equally terrified of what it was and what would happen if she dared glance back. "Think about what you're doing. You don't want to do this! I'm not worth it. You want me out of Havenwood Falls? I'll go! Next bus out, I'm on it! *Just don't kill me*."

The chainsaw sputtered, Guy's thumb edging off the throttle.

"Uh, Octavia? You're going to want to see this." Willie interjected in a surprisingly cavalier tone.

Swallowing hard, Octavia squeezed her eyes shut. "I'm pretty sure I don't," she eeped. Forced back another step, her shoulder slammed into something hard and unyielding. The cold radiating off it skittered through her in ominous warning.

"No, *no*! Whatever it is, I haven't seen it!" Head tilting to the side, Octavia peeled one eye open and risked a peek. "I didn't see your . . . giant ice weenie?"

Chainsaw clicking off, Guy slid his goggles up onto his head. "I didn't hear a word of that. But if you knock over my sculpture, you're fired."

Shuffling in a half circle on the tarp, Octavia sought clarity, yet found only a giant hot dog. Blinking hard, her mind tried to grapple the pieces of that perplexing puzzle into place.

"What . . . the fuck is that?" she asked in the closest she could come to an eloquent response.

A hurt-bunny look creased Guy's features. "I don't claim to be the best, but I thought it was at least recognizable. It's a hot dog in a bun. I've been taking ice sculpting classes at the Annex."

"No, I get that. I do." Octavia nodded with a tad too much enthusiasm (as one would expect mere seconds after thinking they were about to be slaughtered in a horribly bloody fashion). "What I don't get is, why?"

"Last year at the bonfire they bitched about my hot dogs being too big for the damned buns. Well, the cookie crawl is coming up, and *this* will be my ultimate rebuttal to their pettiness. No more words. No more messages on the front window. Just a giant ice dog doing the talking for me." Setting down his chainsaw, he crossed his arms with an indignant snort. "I came down here to do the final touches on the details. Then I was going to wrap it in tarps and use my dolly to load it into the back of my truck."

Pushing himself off the floor, Willie brushed the dirt from his palms. "And I suppose you need duct tape to keep the tarps wrapped around it?"

Guy sized him up with a glare. "Who the hell is this guy?"

"This is my . . ." Octavia searched for a word to describe their relationship, but in that regard, language fell tragically short. Out of options, she went for the obvious. "Willie. This is my Willie."

Hitching one brow, Guy shrugged. "Damn, kids today really just call a spade a spade, don't they? While I'm not one to judge, I would like to know why you're here. I do need to get back to work."

"I . . ." Octavia's mouth opened and shut, looking for some logical explanation for breaking and entering. "Lied. I took the pig. It was me. I still have it. Matter of fact, at this moment, it's probably ruining my bathroom at Whisper Falls Inn. For real. There's a good chance I'm not getting my security deposit back."

"Of course you're not." Guy's face crinkled in disgust. "You left meat rotting in a room temperature location. It's like you're trying to hot box yourself in rancid funk. And for what? Is this some kind of save the animals protest? Because ya can't save 'em when they're already dead."

"That's the thing." Sucking air through her teeth, Octavia's head tilted. "I *can*."

Stunned realization wiped all emotion from the butcher's features. "You're a necromancer."

"I'm a necromancer."

"You brought my pig to life."

"I brought your pig to life."

"It was the pig that pooped in my office, not you during some sort of stomach flu."

"It was the pig that . . . wait. You thought *I* did that? *Ew!*"

Biting his lower lip with his rows of pointed little teeth, Guy glanced toward the stairs. "The Court gave me your file. I never read it. I choose, instead, to judge people by their behavior in the moment. Which is why I find most to be raging assholes. Regardless, if the Court finds out about that pig, you'll be in a world of trouble. I'm sure they already felt the stir of magic. I'm surprised they didn't come to investigate."

"They did." Octavia explained, shoving her hands into the pockets of her puffy winter coat. "I made a steak shimmy. It was a whole thing." With a sideways glance to Willie, she saw her chance at a life in Havenwood Falls slipping away. If Guy wanted her gone, she had just given him all the ammunition he needed. She should be used to this feeling, of being chased from a chance at pseudo-normalcy. Still, the recurring experience never lost its sting.

Guy's thick, wiry brows lifted in surprise. "I'm actually really glad I missed that little show. Still, the pig being alive and restored doesn't change the fact that if the Court finds out, you'll be kicked out of town and the wards strengthened to ensure you never get back in."

Casting her stare to the floor, Octavia bit her lower lip and prepared for the inevitable. "Yeah, that's exactly what would happen."

"Sir, you should know, the pig was my fault." Stepping forward, Willie made a valiant attempt on her behalf. "I scared her, and she fell backwards onto the little guy. What followed was completely an accident."

"Why were you in my freezer?" Guy huffed.

"I'm her boyfriend, and I . . . like to have romantic time there. The harsh bite of cold is . . . uh . . . enticing?" Wearing an apologetic grimace, Willie's voice rose enough at the end to morph into a question.

Guy blinked his way, face reddening with brewing annoyance. Pivoting on his heel, his attention snapped in Octavia's direction.

"Keep him out of the shop. The veal is too young to see that sort of thing."

While Willie's forehead puckered in confusion, Octavia erupted in a loud bark of nervous laughter. When no one joined in, she awkwardly cleared her throat. "It's funny, because it's baby meat."

Ignoring her outburst, Guy pulled his phone from his back pocket and thumbed in a number.

Fearing the worst, Octavia shook her head and frantically waved her hands in front of her. "You don't have to do this. I'll hop on my bike and be gone by—"

"Michaela?" Guy rumbled into the phone. "Guy Pyntz of Pyntz Butcher Shoppe. I need to add a pet rider to Octavia Hollows's room. Mm-hm. Yeah, I gave her a pig. Little bugger was too cute to kill. Her words, not mine. Yeah, that's probably what you're smelling. Although, I wouldn't put it past a guest to be eating ribs in their room. How about if I send over a month's worth of blood, on me, and we call it even? The good stuff from the Aberdeen Angus steer you like? Absolutely. I'll get that over to you tomorrow. Thanks, Michaela." Clicking the phone off, Guy granted her an almost smile. "You paid for the pig. He's yours now."

"I named him Bacon," Octavia muttered in place of the *thank you* she knew would make the hobgoblin bristle.

"Repig and Spam were thrown around," Willie added, rubbing his hands together to warm them.

"People have a lot of misconceptions about me." Unscrewing the gas tank on the chainsaw, Guy checked the fuel level. "Many form their opinions without taking the time to know me. I'm not one to do that to others. You made a mistake. A pink-bellied little mistake. It could have been far worse. Truth is, you've been a welcome addition to the shop, and I'm not ready to lose you."

"I'm not ready to be . . . lost." While moved by the sentiments of the surly little man, Octavia was struck by a wave of apprehension. It wasn't Guy who wanted her gone, which meant they were no closer to finding the murderous entity lurking in Havenwood Falls.

"All right." Giving the cord a firm yank, Guy fired the chainsaw back to life. "Now, get the hell out of my basement and don't come back without an invitation. Not that I have plans to ever extend one."

Octavia tried to duck around Guy, only to smack into Willie trying to take the same narrow path. "I go left, you go right? No? Both right? Oh hell, just follow me."

After stumbling around in a clumsy dance, Octavia grabbed Willie's coat sleeve and tugged him behind her in a wide arc well outside of chainsaw swiping range.

"Oh, and Octavia?" Guy hollered the moment her boot came down on the bottom step. "You open in the morning. I'm going to be up late finishing the detailing. I'm having a hard time getting the right wrinkles at the end of my frankfurter. This could end up being an all-nighter."

Not waiting for a response, Guy turned back to his ice creation. With the edge of the whirring blade, he connected with the block of ice in delicate swipes that sent ice fragments spraying through the air.

"I feel kind of bad we thought that Guy was the killer. All he wanted was to make beautiful weenie art." Octavia's shoulders bobbed with relieved laughter.

"I hate to ruin the moment." Back outside, Willie's breath encircled his face in a wreath of white steam. "But we're out in the open, after dark, in a town full of *literally* every known species that goes bump in the night. Add to that the fact that *someone* wants us both gone, and I'm suddenly feeling very vulnerable and exposed."

The smile dying on her lips, Octavia jerked her head in the direction of her hidden motorcycle. "Let's get back to the inn. We're back to square one with a killer on the loose. That puts us at a terrifying disadvantage."

# CHAPTER 9

Once they were safely back at Whisper Falls Inn, Octavia and Willie were able to find the funny in the night's ordeal.

"Where did he even come from?" Octavia chuckled, unlocking the door to her room. "Was he just waiting behind the furnace?"

Bent in half by a fit of laughter, Willie clapped a hand onto her shoulder. "He was waiting for the right moment to achieve ultimate pint-sized terror."

"Pyntz size! Well played on the pun!" Tumbling into the room, Octavia tried to kick the door shut behind her, only to lose her footing. Spinning around, she latched onto Willie's forearms to steady herself.

Just like that, the situation became far less funny.

Willie's hand raised to catch a lock of her cotton-candy-pink hair that had tangled with her lashes. Dragging two fingers down the rebellious strand, he gave it a gentle tug before tucking it behind her ear. Gaze following the curve of her lips, his pupils dilated with heady desire.

Octavia's head swam with reasons to inject distance between them.

She wasn't over Elba.

She didn't know who Willie really was.

Technically speaking, the dude *had* been recently deceased.

Still, the intensity of his stare awoke a hot longing within her she had thought was long dead. Face tipped to his, Octavia drew in a ragged breath. At that intimate proximity, she could see what looked like a ring of unbreakable titanium surrounding the glimmering silver of his eyes. Flaxen hair fell across his forehead, tempting her to drag her fingers through its silky disarray. His lips parted in delicious invitation, the stubble across his jaw line adding a rough edge to his boy-next-door charm.

So many reasons to say no. Yet, with his breath tingling over her cheeks in hypnotic waves of warmth, every last one of them floated from her mind. Rising on tiptoe, her lips brushed his, asking an unspoken question.

Desire sharpening his features, he snaked his hands around her waist, pulling her to him with gentle insistence. His mouth claimed hers, the heat of his building desire crushing against her thigh. He lifted her from the ground, a low growl rumbling from his throat as her legs locked around his waist.

A dam of stopped-up emotion cracked within her, letting loose the tidal wave of truth Octavia fought to suppress. She told herself she needed no one, that she could survive without love or affection. The pain of losing Elba had been such a soul-crushing one, and a lifetime of loneliness seemed the safe alternative. Yet with Willie nuzzled into the crook of her neck, kissing and nibbling his way to the curve of her collarbone, she acknowledged these as the lies they were.

As he inched Octavia back, the edge of the mattress bumped

Willie's legs, and he lowered her down onto the quilted comforter. They pulled back, their eyes meeting in an electrified pulse.

"My angel of mercy," he murmured against her lips, his fingers wandering under the hem of her puffy coat.

"We're both wearing a lot of layers," Octavia said with a husky chuckle. "We might want to shimmy off a few before one of us accidentally gets to second base with a knitted scarf."

"How could I resist such an invitation?" Pushing off the mattress, Willie sprang to his feet. Unzipping his coat, he dropped it to the floor in a heap. His hat, gloves, and scarf were next to follow.

Scooting back on the bed, Octavia pulled herself up onto her knees. Hitching one brow his way in daring invitation, she bit her lower lip and shrugged off the coat that made her look like a giant blueberry. Shifting her weight to fling it aside, a piece of paper crinkled beneath her knee.

Momentarily tugged out of the moment, she read the words written on it out loud as Willie prowled up the mattress. "Heard your pig rooting around, and took him for a walk to get some real food. FYI, popcorn isn't pig chow. I'll bring him back soon. Also, Madame Luiza felt a presence attempting to manifest somewhere in the inn. You may want to do a sage smudging ritual to cleanse your room. I'll show you how when I do the other rooms tomorrow. See you soon, Michaela."

Hand encircling her ankle, Willie tugged her beneath him. With his mouth teasing over the delicate skin of her neck, he rolled his hips to position himself between her thighs.

"Your pillow talk leaves something to be desired." Propping himself up on one elbow, Willie's opposite hand thumbed the buttons free on her flannel shirt.

Octavia wadded up the note and threw it in the general direction of the garbage can. Wetting her lips, she weaved her hands around Willie's neck. "Really, though, is there anything worse than pig parent-shaming? He loves popcorn!"

Parting the fabric of her shirt, he traced the delicate stitching of her black cotton bra with the side of his knuckle. "While I'm grateful we have a pig-sitter, I feel I need to work a little harder to get your head in the game."

His hand traveled down the length of her arm, fingers lacing with hers. Bringing her hand to his lips, he kissed each finger one by one, then raised her arm over her head, pinning her hand to the mattress while his mouth teased down her torso.

Eyes closed, Octavia expelled a throaty sigh of appreciation. It was then that a slight flicker of green caught her attention from behind her fluttering lashes. Head lolling to the side, she gazed over with casual interest.

Blinking in festering confusion, the breath lodged in her throat. Brow knit tight, she glanced from their twined hands to the top of Willie's head, and back again.

*No, it couldn't be.*

Emerald light crackled over Willie's skin, sparking and snapping in time with his racing heart.

*His* skin.

Not hers.

As if summoned by her startling realization, Elba's ghostly form shimmered into view, filling the bathroom doorway.

"*Wrong guy,*" he rasped, using the force of his energy to knock over the leather satchel Willie's clothes were found in.

It slumped to the side, allowing an orange pill bottle to roll out.

"Did you say something?" Cheeks ruddy with desire, Willie glanced up from his task of peppering kisses around her navel.

Not bothering with an attempt at explanation, Octavia shoved him aside to wriggle off the bed.

"Octavia, what's wrong?" Sitting up, Willie combed his fingers through his tousled hair.

Haunted by the chill of Elba once more vanishing from sight, Octavia crouched down to collect the bottle.

"Octavia?" Willie tried again.

Turning her find label up, Octavia read it out loud. "Pierce Pennington; one milligram Xanax. No refills."

Dragging his palm over the stubble of his chin, Willie feigned indifference. It would have been convincing too, had it not been for the ruddy flush creeping up his neck. "Yeah, I found that in that bag. I probably should have told you about it. Yet another piece to this unsolved mystery."

Stabbing her hand into the satchel, she pulled out a wallet he said hadn't been there to begin with. Flipping it open, she confirmed her developing theory. With two fingers she extracted her crucial piece of evidence. "That's funny. Here's the driver's license of a Mr. Pierce Pennington. He looks an awful lot like you, wouldn't you say?"

With a flick of her wrist, she tossed the ID onto the bed beside him. Clutching the pill bottle in her closed fist, Octavia waited for the next lie to tumble from his lips.

Instead of reaching for the license, Willie stared down at it like it was a venomous serpent. "Octavia, this isn't what you think it is."

"Oh, yeah?" Flames of fury smoldering in her glare, Octavia's top lip curled into a sneer. "So, you *didn't* walk into the freezer all by yourself? It wasn't *you* who neatly folded your clothes and shoved them into that bag before swallowing a handful of your own prescription medication? Because, from where I'm standing, it looks like you staged this *entire thing*. Hell, I bet you even set off the town's wards when you entered. Every supernatural does. But you offing yourself took your own blip of magic off the radar before anyone could investigate, *and* probably made them even more suspicious of *me*!"

Kicking his legs off the edge of the bed, Willie—no, Pierce—rested his elbows on his knees and peered up at her from under his lashes. "Why would I do that? What sense would it make to take such an unnecessary risk?"

Pulling herself up to her full height, Octavia ground her teeth to the point of pain. "Because . . . you're a necromancer. Just. Like. Me."

To his credit, Willie achieved an impressively convincing dumbfounded grin. "What? Why would you say that?"

"I'm guessing you've never gotten freaky with another necromancer before." Taking a threatening step closer, Octavia glared down at him. "It was a first for me, too. But see, whatever-the-hell-your-name-is, in the heat of the moment more than that lump of flesh in your pants made its presence known."

Willie shook his head like she was spouting gibberish. "What?"

"A green current was pulsing over your knuckles. The same sort of energy that shoots from my palms every time I bring someone or something back." Folding her arms over her chest, she glowered down at him. "I'm sure you have another cleverly crafted excuse for that. So, let's hear it. Go ahead. Explain it away. You seem to have a talent for that."

"Octavia, *you're* the necromancer. It was probably *your* energy you saw. I mean, you were pretty worked up, too." Pushing off the bed, Willie reached for her, only to have Octavia shrug away from his touch.

Raising her hands between them, Octavia curled them into tight fists. "I have been on my own since I was *fourteen*. I know, all too well, when I'm being played. *Tell me the truth*."

A cloak of silence fell, broken only by the bedsprings squeaking under Willie as he shifted his weight. "You've been alone, for so long," he murmured to the carpet beneath his feet. "All I ever wanted was to offer you a chance at a family . . . at *forever.*"

"You not remembering your name, was that complete bullshit?" Octavia's voice reached her own ears in an unsteady tremble she didn't recognize. "Was all of that amnesia stuff part of the act?"

Hair falling forward to shield his eyes, Willie nodded. "My name *is* Pierce. I was born to a wealthy pair of warlocks who used a pure-bred witch as their surrogate. They schooled me in our ways and traditions from birth and were thrilled beyond compare when the strength of my abilities revealed itself to be in necromancy. They called the most skilled shamans in the world in to train me." A look of awe stole over his features as he gazed up at her. "Still, I could never *touch* the power you possess. I can restore life for a short while. Even then, it's severely limited. My specimens can grunt but not talk, shuffle but not stride. Not once have I been able to restore any kind of mental functions. Not like you, with your mind-blowing artistry."

That familiar feeling, of being the star of a freak show, skittered up Octavia's spine. "You knew who I was when you came here? That's why you staged all of this?"

"I came here for you." Sliding off the bed, Willie/Pierce fell to his knees before her. "I've tracked you since the school shooting. What you did there was . . . *amazing.* You gave those kids their lives back, even if your gift was stolen away far too soon! Ever since then, I've been watching and waiting for the perfect moment to arrange our 'chance' meeting. Your power blows me away. No, *you* blow me away! You stepping foot in town triggered every ward in place, while I was able to walk in and do what I needed to do before anyone noticed me as much more than another ski bunny in a tourist town. Your power announces you as the queen you are. All you had to do was touch Bacon, and me, to revive us. It takes me channeling every ounce of my will to accomplish a *fraction* of what you can. Please, Octavia, you've been alone for so long. *Let me be with you.* It's all I ask, all I want. Imagine what we could accomplish together. We could raise an undead army and own this town. Hell, we could own *any* town! The world could be ours . . . if you would just say yes."

Chewing on her lower lip, Octavia's heart pounded in her temples, hammering in like railroad spikes. "You've been watching me? For years?"

Gathering her hands in his, Willie showered her flesh with kisses. "I've been waiting for you to be ready and open to the possibility of *us.* For so long, something or someone was always in the way. All of that is changed now. Finally, we can be together."

Snatching her hands free from his grasp, a fist of icy reality closed around Octavia's throat. The only words she could manage came out as little more than a choked whisper. "In the way? Elba was killed in an accident on one of his construction sites. Did you . . . have anything to do with that?"

Arms falling limp at his sides, Willie's crumpled expression pleaded for her understanding. "Everything I have ever done, I did for us. Because I love you."

"You don't know me! Now answer the fucking question! Did you have anything to do with it?" she demanded, the harshness of her words slicing to bone.

Rocking back, he pushed to his feet. Striding to the window, Pierce stared out at the sleepy town blanketed by night. "He wasn't right for you. There I was, following you from town to town, just waiting for my chance. He showed up with that big smile and even bigger dreams, and completely spun you." Chin tilting in her direction, Willie weighed his words carefully. "He offered you normalcy. You know as well as I do that kind of life would never fit you. What I did was a mercy to him as much as to you."

Eyes burning with the threat of tears, Octavia's teeth clenched in a vicious snarl. "What. Did. You. Do?"

His attention drawn back to the window, the darkness became his confessional. "I volunteered on the job site just to learn more about the man who stole your heart. I had to know what it was about him, why it was you fell so hard. Truth be told, I never did figure that out. You should know, it wasn't my intention to harm him. But the opportunity presented itself like a perfectly wrapped gift."

Hand fluttering to her mouth, Octavia stifled a sob.

"The scaffolding was already wobbly under the weight of the bags of concrete stacked on top of it." Tone absent of emotion, Willie recounted the story as if it was nothing more than something he happened upon in a news article. "All it took was a bump, and the entire structure collapsed on him. Clearly, the site wasn't up to OSHA standards. I wager there were some hefty fines after that." Turning to face her, Pierce/Willie's eyebrows raised in challenge. "That said, if you loved him so much, why didn't you bring him back? All it would have taken was a touch."

"You know why!" Octavia's fingernails dug half-moons into her palms. "What we do is an affront to the natural order of things!"

Glee glittering in the silver-laced pools of his stare, Willie clucked his tongue against the roof of his mouth. "And you let that stop you? That's a shame. Maybe you didn't love him as much as you claim."

"His body was gone!" Octavia screamed until her throat ached, unleashing the truth that had haunted her from one new city to the next. "I broke into the funeral home to wake him up, but he was already gone! All they buried during his funeral was a weighted box of rocks!"

Triumph puffed Willie's chest, as if he had provided adequate proof for her to accept what she was. "See? There it is. The part of you that wants to flip off all that natural order bullshit and embrace what you truly are."

Feeling that familiar charge building in her core, Octavia washed her face of emotion to distract from the emerald sparks rippling up and down the length of her arms.

"You're right. I *am* a giver of life. I restore what others cannot, crossing the threshold of what many consider to be impossible. No spells or incantations could ever accomplish what I can. You want my power for some greater plan?" Slow and steady, she closed the space between them until she stood toe to toe with the man who snuffed out her chance at love.

Pupils dilated with desire, he rasped, "I want *all* of you."

Octavia's hands shot out before he could so much as flinch, catching Willie's wrists in an ironclad grip. "You want it? You've got it, you son of a bitch. Take it. *Take it all!*"

Focusing her energy, she slammed every bit of her power into him in a tidal wave of cresting green current. Her hair blew back in licking pink strands, lashing her cheeks a brilliant red. Instead of pulling away, Willie leaned into her pulsing jolts. Fingers curling around her forearms, his head fell back at the euphoric rush coursing into him. What started as roils of ecstasy murmured through parted lips soon morphed into a tortured shriek ripping from his lungs. With Octavia's gifted touch of life came years of age. Time ravaged over his weakening form. Skin sagged. Hair bleached white. Eyes sunk in their sockets. Flesh cracked and crumbled into a pillar of dust before exploding out to cover every surface in the room.

Silence fell with the finality of a coffin lid.

Sinking to the floor, Octavia dragged a hand over her face to wipe away the soot and grime. Each inhale hurt more than the last. Not from the polluted air, but because the scab on her fragile heart had been ripped off, exposing the festering wound beneath.

Ravaged by emotion, her shoulders shook with each sob. Tears streamed zigzag paths down her dust covered cheeks.

"I'm sorry, Elba," she sniveled to the empty room. "I never should have given up. I should have spent the rest of my days looking for you. Loving me was the only mistake you ever made, and it cost you your life. Baby . . . I'm so sorry."

He appeared to her haloed by light, looking more an ethereal essence than his earlier haunting presence. Brown skin aglow with flawless beauty, Elba granted her a loving smile that seemed to hold every mystery of the universe. "Retrace your steps. You'll find me somewhere between where you are and where we were together. Come and find me, Octavia. Bring me home."

"I can't!" Her hands reached for him, swiping nothing but misty air. "I don't know how! Too much time has passed."

Granting her a smile of heartfelt devotion, Elba beseeched her once more. "Bring me . . . home."

With that, he was gone.

# CHAPTER 10

"There you go. One bacon-bourbon hot cocoa." Forcing a smile her heart didn't feel, Octavia handed over the delectable treat to yet another customer taking part in the Havenwood Falls Hot Cocoa & Cookie Crawl.

Dressed up in its holiday finest, the beautiful town square had been transformed into a winter wonderland. The businesses spared no expense on their decorations, and threw their doors open wide to welcome guests for holiday treats and merriment. The sidewalks were filled with smiling faces and rosy cheeks, the sound of Christmas carols filling the air.

Octavia's heart longed to join in the joyful celebration of the season. Unfortunately, she couldn't get past the pestering feeling that there was somewhere else she needed to be. Turning her back to the windows, she treated herself to a sip of the bourbon in hopes of quieting the internal nagging of her mind. After all, what it was steering her toward was impossible. Wasn't it?

"See?" Guy nodded toward the brown bottle in her hand. "Having a little nip of that makes it a little better to be here after business hours."

Handing the bourbon to her pint-sized boss, Octavia leaned the small of her back against the cutting counter. "That's what was behind your prize-winning cocoa recipe? Merely tolerating people? I thought it had more to do with keeping the swarms of kids out of here."

"That's the truth of it! This place is full of knives and glass!" Guy erupted, the amber colored liquid sloshing from the bottle as he talked with his hands in wild gestures. "They come in here and smear every shiny surface with their dirty little hands."

"And the truth shall set you free." Octavia chuckled at his outburst.

A happy little snort drew their attention toward the backroom, where Bacon trotted out, head held high to show off the Santa hat Guy bought for his favorite swine. Having a pet pig as the makeshift mascot for the butcher shop proved great for business, and would provide the townspeople plenty of inspiration for the purple pig plate painting in the park in the spring. Word spread quickly through town about their sweet little four-legged friend, prompting people to come in for the sole purpose of giving Bacon a scratch on the chin, only to leave with thirty dollars' worth of meat. Needless to say, that rise in sales had swayed Bacon into Guy's favor in a big way.

"Speaking of the truth . . ." Setting the bottle of bourbon aside, Guy shuffled to the crockpot full of cocoa to give the chocolatey goodness that had settled to the bottom a stir. "Are you ever going to tell me what happened to that fella of yours? The one that admitted to being in my freezer?"

"He wasn't my fella," Octavia snapped. Hearing the sharpness of her tone, she cleared her throat and tried to manage a more even keel. "Turns out, I didn't really know him at all. He's . . . gone."

It had taken a thorough vacuuming and washing her bedding three times at the laundromat, but that sentiment was very true. Any trace of Willie—or whoever he was—was gone from her life. Of course, her magical burst was felt. The Court sent Mathilde Augustine over to investigate. With no body, no blood, no signs of anything except a room that needed to be dusted, they could find no violation of her probation. Still, Octavia feared the guilt over what had transpired would cast a dark shadow over her heart that she would never truly escape. His attempt to set her up and convince her to join his twisted cause had failed. Still, somewhere out there he had parents who cared for him, who would wonder what had become of their boy. Add to that the fact that they were powerful warlocks, and Octavia had no doubt this matter was far from over. The most she could be grateful for was that the Court hadn't learned of the staged slip-up, and she was safe—for now.

As if cued by Octavia's troubled thoughts, the door chimed. Addie strolled in, her cheeks red from the sharp bite of the winter wind. "It's not a Hot Cocoa & Cookie Crawl without a bacon-bourbon hot cocoa! Fix it up, Guy, and don't be stingy with the bacon."

"Double bourbon, double bacon. Coming right up." Guy snorted, chin dipping in a nod as he swiveled to fill her order. "Did you see my ice sculpture outside? Do you think those whine-tits from last year got the point?"

"I think, as weenie art goes, it's lovely." Glancing to Octavia, Addie rolled her eyes at the gruff hobgoblin. "And that you *really* need to learn to let things go. Octavia, you should get some sort of medal for putting up with him day in and day out."

"Ah, he's not so bad." Octavia grinned, jamming her thumb in the direction of the booze bottle. "Especially on the days he lets me drink on the job."

"Well, I hope you haven't had *too* many pulls off that thing, because you and I have important business to discuss." Adjusting her beanie cap to better cover her ears, Addie's eyes twinkled with delight.

"What's that?" Octavia asked, passing Guy the chocolate sprinkles and cinnamon to top off his cocoa concoction.

"I have been sent with a very important message from the Court. As of today, *you* are officially off probation." Rising up on the balls of her feet, Addie reached over the counter to accept her cocoa from Guy. "You are welcome to become a resident of Havenwood Falls! I can even make your tattoo permanent. Maybe another night on that last part, though. Incantations and liquor don't mix well. That's how you end up with a tail that matches Bacon's."

While handling payment for the cocoa, Guy and Addie both kept their expectant stares locked on Octavia, waiting for her jubilant reaction.

Instead, she froze, struggling to blink her way through tumultuous thoughts.

"I said that out loud, right?" Addie muttered to Guy out of the corner of her mouth. "Truth be told, the girls and I pre-gamed the crawl with cider spiked with butterscotch schnapps, so I may have just thought it at her. That tactic only really works on Elsmed Fairchild."

"No, you said it all right. And this is the first time I've ever seen her stop talking." Guy's mouth fell into a downward C of impressed appreciation. "Whatever magic caused this wonderful turn of events, I'm going to need you to teach me."

Treating herself to a sip of the hot chocolate left Addie with a foamy whipped-cream mustache she wiped away with her thumb and forefinger. "What's wrong? You seemed to be settling in so well. I thought you'd be thrilled to call our little village home."

"I am, and I *do* want that," Octavia admitted, dragging one hand over her face as if the gesture could somehow clear away her fog of confusion. "I just . . . I think there's something I have to do first. I left some things from my past unsettled outside of Havenwood Falls. Before I can put down roots here, I have to make sure I'm doing it free from questions or regret."

A knowing smile stole over Addie's features, softening them with an affectionate glow. "Let me guess—this somehow involves a certain ghostly boyfriend who led you here?"

Octavia didn't even ask how she knew. In this town, a thread of magic weaved them all together in one way or another. "Thanks to the added focus you gave me with that tattoo, I think I may finally be able to find him and get a little closure. Put that part of my life to rest, once and for all. Goddess knows, my battered heart could sure as hell use it."

With a humorless huff of laughter, Guy shook his head and handed Addie her change over the counter.

"Oh, sweet girl." Addie clucked her tongue against the roof of her mouth like that was the most adorably clueless thing she had ever heard. "That tattoo had nothing to do with your focus or control. The only thing I threw in, other than the basics I give to any supe, was a touch of self-confidence, of which you were sorely lacking. Whatever control or boost you feel it gave you was in you from the start."

That news hit Octavia hard enough to momentarily knock the entire English language clean out of her head.

"You managed to silence her *twice* within a matter of minutes. That earns a second cocoa on the house!" Guy grunted, his lips peeling back into a grin that revealed the canine incisors on his protruding lower jaw.

"Woo! We're gonna put the crawl in Cookie Crawl tonight! And I'm definitely in sore need of it." Addie hooted, slapping her free hand on the countertop. "Before I get my bourbon goggles on, I should give you the small print terms if you're going to leave town.

If you want to come back, you're going to need your resident tattoo. Otherwise, the second you leave town, you'll forget all about us. As a resident, you'll still only retain your memories of Havenwood Falls and all that happened here for a lunar cycle. Miss that deadline, and we all become a time in your life you can't quite recall. The second you step outside of the wards, the clock is running. You'll have twenty-eight days to do what you need to do, and get back. I'll be back in the morning to give you your *permanent* tattoo." Double-fisting her hot chocolates, Addie strolled to the door and pushed it open with her back. "Thanks for these, Guy. And, congratulations, Octavia. I knew from the beginning you would fit right in! I guess this is the part where I say welcome home!"

# CHAPTER 11

*T*he next morning, with her resident tattoo in place, Octavia made up her mind and checked out of Whisper Falls Inn, a decision that was made somewhat easier by an unexplainable magical surge she felt the night before. It was the kind she only felt when things were about to take a particularly ghoulish turn, and it made the packing process fractionally less melancholy. Everything she owned, sans Bacon, had been shoved back into her backpack. While she was taking nothing extra with her, the role of traveling vagabond seemed a tighter fit than before.

With her motorcycle parked at the curb outside Pyntz Butcher Shoppe, she braced herself for a reluctant goodbye.

"One month," Guy grumbled, shoving his stubby hands into the pockets of his flannel-lined Carhartt. "Your job will be waiting for you. Hurry back."

Kicking her leg over the bike, Octavia settled on the cold, stiff leather. "Aw, are you going to miss me?"

"Hell no!" he huffed, his brow furrowing into a deep V. "I got used to not having to deal with people at the shop. I want you to get your ass back here, so I can go back to not having to talk to shitheels."

"Truly a sweet sentiment." Octavia chuckled as she slid on her helmet. "Really, someone should cross-stitch that onto a pillow."

Chewing on the inside of his cheek, Guy eyed the motorcycle as if questioning its reliability and mechanics. "What's your plan?"

"Elba's spirit said something about finding him between here and where we last were together. So I'm going to retrace my steps, town to town, until I get back to Tallahassee, where he died." Lifting her chin, she snapped her helmet strap into place. "Hopefully, I'll find things along the way that will lead me back to him."

"And if it doesn't?"

"Then I can come back knowing I tried my damnedest."

"A month isn't long—"

"I can do it," Octavia interrupted.

Stepping forward, he laid his hand over hers. "It isn't long, and shit can happen. I will call you every day, even if it's just to hear that annoying whine you call a voice. You may forget the town, but you'll never lose me, kid."

Chewing on the inside of her cheek, Octavia blinked away the burn of threatening tears. "Good, because I don't know what I would do without you around to give me hell."

Snorting his satisfaction with her answer, Guy pulled a package out from behind his back and jammed it in her direction. "I got you something."

Shaking off her gloves, Octavia tentatively reached for the package wrapped in plain white butcher paper. "It isn't going to explode, is it?"

"Quit with the lip and open it."

Tearing it open, she found herself holding up straps of nylon fabric and reading the tag for some clue as to what she was looking at. "Cuddlebug Infant Carrier. I would say thank you, but I legit have no idea what this is."

"There's more." Snatching the box out of her grip, Guy dug out a child's size helmet and sunglasses, which he proudly held up for her to see.

"Yet somehow that leaves me with more questions than answers," she mused.

"You buckle this on yourself," Guy explained, pantomiming strapping it around his middle. "Then, you can nestle Bacon right in there at your chest, and have a safe way for him to travel with you."

"And you even thought to protect his little undead pig brain with a helmet." Octavia tsked. "You're just the best pig-pa ever."

Guy paused in scooping up Bacon to shoot a glare in her direction. "Don't call me that. I just didn't want to get stuck taking care of your swine."

After buckling the strap around her waist, Octavia held open the infant pouch-seat, so Guy could guide Bacon into place. Not only did he make sure the piglet was safe and comfortable, he also took the time to top off biker-pig's look with the snazzy sunglasses.

"I *might* have believed you just wanted him gone, had you *not* bought him his own pair of nifty aviator shades."

Unable to argue with the truth, the gruff hobgoblin peered up at her with paternal concern. "Be safe out there, and call me if you need *anything*."

"I will." Knowing if she didn't leave then, she wouldn't go at all, Octavia fired the bike to life. "I'll see you soon. I promise."

Taking a step back, Guy's face folded into a stern scowl. "I'm holding you to that."

Leaning the motorcycle away from the curb, Octavia roared off with a knot in her gut. For the first time in her life, she felt at home. Yet, there she was, steering away from her chance at community and family. She had to trust she would find her way back in time. Failure wasn't an option.

The main road out of town twined up into the mountains, allowing a beautiful view of all she was leaving behind. Mountains and trees, as far as the eye could see. Unable to resist, Octavia pulled onto the gravel shoulder to gaze down at the picturesque little burg she had come to love.

"One month," she muttered to Bacon, offering him a light scratch on the snout. "Think we can find Elba in time?"

The contently cuddled little pig gave a supportive snort in response.

Octavia grinned down at his pointed little ears poking out from beneath the helmet gifted by his pig-pa.

"Me too." Easing her thumb off the clutch, she allowed her beast of a bike to roll on. "Let's ride."

We hope you enjoyed this story in the Havenwood Falls series featuring a variety of supernatural creatures. The series is a collaborative effort by multiple authors.

Books you might also enjoy in the main Havenwood Falls series:

*The Winged & the Wicked* by T.V. Hahn & Kristie Cook
*Nowhere to Hide* by Belinda Boring
*Defying Gravity* by Kallie Ross
*The Lurkers Within* by Danielle Bannister

Also look for the YA line, Havenwood Falls High; the historical paranormal line, Legends of Havenwood Falls; the sexier side of town, Havenwood Falls Sin & Silk; the local supernatural college, Sun & Moon Academy; and the Havenwood Falls holiday short story anthologies.

Stay up to date at www.HavenwoodFalls.com

# ABOUT THE AUTHOR

- Utopia Award Winner Author of the Year 2018
- Utopia Award Winner for Best Villain 2018 for Ursula in *Rise of the Sea Witch*
- Readers' Favorite YA Fantasy Bronze Medal Winner 2017
- Readers' Favorite Fantasy Silver Medal Winner for 2015
- Turning Pages Magazine Winner for Best YA book of 2013 & Best Teen Book of 2013
- RONE Award Winner for Best YA Paranormal Work of 2012
- Young Adult and Teen Reader voted Author of the Year 2012

Stacey Rourke is the award-winning author of works that span genres, but possess the same flair for action and snarky humor. She lives in Florida with her husband, two beautiful daughters, and two giant dogs. Stacey loves to travel, has an unhealthy shoe addiction, and considers herself blessed to make a career out of talking to the imaginary people that live in her head.

Visit her at www.staceyrourke.com
On Facebook at
www.facebook.com/staceyrourkeauthor
or on Twitter or Instagram @Rourkewrites.

# AN EXCERPT

~ A Havenwood Falls New Adult Novella ~

# Havenwood Falls

## THE LURKERS WITHIN

### DANIELLE BANNISTER

### *The Lurkers Within* (A Havenwood Falls Novella) by Danielle Bannister

Spirit Agent Tasha Young has never fit in. Her talents as a modern-day ghostbuster make her a loner by necessity. Her job is an easy one. Enter a haunted house, remove the misbehaving spirit, collect the cash, and move on to the next city. When she and her team are invited to Havenwood Falls for a special case, she quickly discovers that this retrieval isn't a simple bag and tag.

What lurks within is not one aura, but hundreds, and they all have their sights set on Tasha. With only five traps in her possession and a team member already sucked into the spirit world, Tasha is forced to come face to face with her greatest enemy: the Indrori.

If she can't find her way out of the spirit realm in time, the Indrori will win the prize he's been waiting centuries to claim. The future of Tasha, her team, and all of Havenwood Falls rests on the sultry black-haired beauty with the snake tattoo.

# THE LURKERS WITHIN

"Want me to take point?" Adam asked. His trap was raised high, like you might raise a gun going into a drug bust. His muscles flexed, showing delicious chocolate biceps. There were no two ways about it—that man was fine, but also not on my radar. Poor boy wanted some quaint Christian girl. That's definitely not me.

"No need," I said. "It's only a Class C spirit. It's not going anywhere."

Generally speaking, Class C spirits were harmless and confined to the places where they died, unless they were way older than this dipshit ghost, who chose to spend his afterlife tormenting a politician. We had him right where we wanted.

I was the last thing a pissed off ghost wanted to see, for good reason, too. I was the best spirit agent around. When a spirit felt me walk into a room, they knew their time was up. What can I say? I was infamous for being a bitch in both the human and spiritual realms. I wouldn't apologize for my skills. Or for being the best in my field. I was paid quite well by the feds for handling these "classified" cases. My job was simple: enter a haunted house, remove the misbehaving spirit, collect the cash, and move on to the next city. The world was none the wiser as to just how many ghosts they walked the earth with. Most were harmless. I only went after the ones that became a problem.

My team was called in this morning to remove a less-than-friendly Casper. This one was trapped in the attic. In a matter of minutes, the job would be over, and I could go back to the hotel, where I planned to sink into their hot tub. It really was the world's easiest job.

More often than not, I got assigned a Class B spirit. Those assholes became strong enough to emit sounds but were mostly harmless. Sure, I might end up with a scratch or two from the older ones, but those went away by the end of a day. Because they were so powerless, demonic spirits specialized in the psychological mind-game damage they could do to the humans they'd been forced to live with. This type of auras wrongly blamed humans for the reasons they were trapped between realms. These were the douchebags I specialized in. Grumpy spirits who liked to bite. That didn't scare me. I was into the rough stuff.

"Room is clear. Waiting on your call, Agent Young," the voice in my headpiece said. Ah, Winston was on today's mission. How wonderful. He was scared shitless of me. As he should have been.

"We go in when I say we go in, Winston."

Winston bumbled an apology, and I focused back on the door.

Beside me, Adam and my other team member, Eduardo, were all business, their traps poised and ready. They were so serious on these missions. For them, I imagined, this was pretty scary shit. Going up against a spirit wasn't as simple for them, mostly because they couldn't see them the way I could. The imagination was always worse than reality when it came to fear. I could see what I was after, so ghosts didn't frighten me in the least. The rest of the world was less fortunate.

To be clear, I couldn't see a ghost in the same way I could see a human. Spirits were not of this realm anymore, and therefore didn't hold the same shape as living, breathing humans. Instead, I saw the fragments of what was left of them—their auras. Their souls. It was sort of like looking at humans with heat-seeking glasses. A blob of pulsing energy. It wasn't crystal clear, but it was enough to be able to aim a trap accurately.

This baddie in the attic would be a cake walk. Normally, I wouldn't be called in for such an easy bag and tag but when this spirit took up residency at a VIP's place, my team was called in by the feds. Of course, if the FBI was asked about its Soul Searcher program and my place on it, it would deny any and all knowledge of me and the other spirit agents. Such was the risk of a confidential job. I was like a ghost myself. Now you see me, now you don't.

Only a few dozen teams like mine existed around the world, though most of them didn't have a team member like me. They had to rely on malfunctioning gadgets and incompetent tech to bring a spirit down. They didn't actually remove the spirit permanently. They simply pushed them somewhere else, but that wasn't my concern.

There were only five of us that the feds had in their employment who were also Recoverers. There were likely dozens more, but none of them wanted to be controlled by the bureaucracy. I didn't mind. It paid well. Being a Recoverer was another special skill of mine. I could bring back the recently crossed over. Well, I could bring them back if I could get to them within a few hours. I couldn't bring back anyone long dead like Elvis or Prince, though I totally would if I could.

Hell, a lot of those "near-death experiences" you read about? Nine times out of ten, it wasn't a miracle. It was a Recoverer sent to bring the soul back to the human realm. These souls weren't fully dead. They were stuck in the spirit realm and hadn't officially crossed over. Like purgatory, I guess. We snatched them out of the waiting rooms of death to live another day. I'd like to say why we brought back who we did had to do with noble reasons like true love, or they had the formula to cure cancer, or some shit like that, but it was usually because they owed money to the mob or were a family member of someone important. The feds charged a pretty penny for a recovery and only those with power could pay it.

I was recovering more souls than I trapped these days. It's like all the Recoverers decided to go on vacation at the same time. Lazy fuckers. No one had a strong work ethic anymore. But that was just fine by me. I'd happily take their fees.

Just then, Eduardo lifted his trap as he winked at me. Unlike Adam, he got off on this part of the gig. He knew the men on this team were there only for show. I was the star, and he liked seeing me in action. Well, Eduardo liked seeing every aspect of me.

I don't say I was the star player merely because of my ability to see the spirits and bring back the dead, though those were pretty kick-ass skills. No, I was the leader of the team because I was the only one who could actually use the trap properly. I don't know if they were just slow on the trigger, aimed wrong, if their guns weren't calibrated right, or what. Whatever the reason, whatever the job, my traps were the only ones that took the spirits down. Adam and Eduardo were basically my backup dancers. I didn't need them at my side, but it sure made an intimidating picture to the spirit.

Nodding, I gave Adam the signal to kick down the attic door. Did we need to break the door to get to the spirit? Hell no. Breaking shit was for the politician's benefit. Might as well make him believe it was harder than it looked, right? Smoke and mirrors. That's all ghost hunting and politics were, after all.

Adam went in first, followed by Eduardo. Each of them shouted for the ghost to show itself. This was really quite a ridiculous thing to say to a ghost, especially with me on the job, but it made them feel useful and masculine to yell.

The ghost was there, plain as day to me. Eduardo and Adam watched my face to follow where I was looking, so they would know where to aim their traps. Usually, I had to walk around to find the thing cowering in a corner, but this spirit was hovering right in front of me. Almost as if it wanted to be found. In fact, I swear it cocked its head when it saw me.

"Why, hello," I said with a smirk.

Adam and Eduardo raised their traps to where I was focused, but my trap remained at my side as I studied the boldness of the spirit. This was unusual behavior for a spirit. They were typically more skittish when they knew their time was up. Color me intrigued.

"Fire?" Adam whispered when I stalled the command.

"Not yet. I need to check on one thing first," I said, tapping against my earpiece. My eyes never left the aura. Though I couldn't see actual eyes, I had the sneaking suspicion its focus was directly on me as well.

"Go ahead, Agent Young," Winston said in my earpiece.

"Is my room ready at the Ritz?"

"Yes. I have booked a king bed, just like you asked."

"Good," I purred. "Eduardo and I plan on making good use of it later." There was a silence on the other end of the com, which assured me I had made poor Winston blush. I knew full well all our conversations during missions were recorded. I didn't say such things to torment Winston, but to annoy my commanding officer, Agent Duncan. He didn't care for the fact that Eduardo and I were screwing around. It was jealousy, pure and simple. They all got that way when I tired of them.

"I suppose it's time to trap this spirit and go play, eh, Eduardo?" I whispered into his ear.

His lips curled into a mischievous smile for a half a second, but then he refocused on the mission, like a good boy.

I lifted my trap in one fluid movement, waiting for the spirit to make a run for it, but it didn't move. It held its ground in front of me. Smart spirit. It would have been wasted energy trying to escape from me.

"Your time is coming," the female-sounding spirit said, though only I could hear it. I raised my eyebrows, impressed in spite of myself. They normally couldn't communicate. It took too much energy. Those four words likely drained her completely. She was easy prey now. Not that she wasn't before.

"Yeah, yeah, we all meet our maker soon enough. Right now, though, it's your turn," I said, before walking right up to her. I pointed the gun to where her head was and pulled the trigger. My wrist singed a bit from the kickback of the gun, but it was a small price to pay.

"Target acquired."

I handed the trap to Adam, who held onto it like it was worth more than gold. Spirits fascinated him. He longed to be able to see them as I did. He always took meticulous notes after each capture, begging me to describe each spirit in as much detail as possible. Apparently, saying it looked like colored smoke wasn't enough for him. I wished he could see an aura, just once, so he'd get off my back about them.

Eduardo was less professional about the completion of our mission and opted to grab my ass instead. He pulled me close for a congratulatory kiss. I wasn't about to object. That man knew how to use his tongue.

"Get a room," Adam groaned. Eduardo and I did this sort of thing all the time, so you'd think he'd be used to it by now, but his prudish ways always left me feeling a little dirty. In the good way.

"Great idea," I said. I'd had enough work for one day. It was well past time to let off some steam. Eduardo was the perfect way to do it, too. We left the attic, arm in arm, leaving all thoughts of the job behind.

Three months and nine captured spirits later, I still wasn't tired of Eduardo, which was a record for me. I don't know if it was because he was Latino and knew how to treat a woman, or if I might have been falling for him. It had to be the first option. I didn't fall for anyone. I left them too soon to allow for that. Eduardo made me break my own rule of no more than two dates. Working with a guy you were also sleeping with, however, complicated that rule. It wasn't as though I could just disappear from his life, like I did with every other guy. It was easy to ditch guys I met when we traveled. Our team was never in one spot for more than a few days. Eduardo was a harder man to shake because he was paid to follow me.

This thing with him was getting out of hand, though. I had to cut this off. I couldn't be the monogamous partner he wanted. That just wasn't me. I was too much of a flirt. After our Thanksgiving break, I'd call it off. It wasn't fair to him. I'd spend the week screwing his brains out, then I'd toss him to the curb. It was a solid plan.

That's when I felt his hands press warmly against my breasts. The way he breathed hot against my neck alerted me to the fact that our morning coffee was about to be postponed.

"You're up early," I teased, reaching my hand around to help him achieve his full potential.

"I say we skip the gym and do our morning workout in bed," he murmured.

"You riding me sounds so much better than me riding the elliptical," I said in my husky voice that drove him wild.

For the next half hour or so, we "worked out" so hard it would have made even Jane Fonda proud. When we had finished, he rolled off me, slapping me on the ass as he did. He was still frisky. Good.

"Hey, Tasha, how many scales do you have filled in now?" Eduardo asked, running his hand along my back, which displayed an outlined tattoo of a Mexican King serpent. It really was an impressive piece of work. My torso held much of the snake's body as it wrapped twice around me. The tail ended at my hairline on the back of my neck while the black head of it disappeared into my 'Garden of Eden.' The individual scales, numbering over a hundred, were outlined and waiting to be fully inked in. A full-body tat like this would likely take twenty or more years to fill in. In its outline form, however, it still made for an epic piece.

"How many? Um . . . a lot." I laughed as I watched his eyes rake over my naked body. I'd lost count of how many were completed, since I started with the ones on my back first. I hated needles and really didn't want to watch it being done, so being face down for as much of the process as possible was ideal. For someone not keen on needles, perhaps a full-body tattoo was stupid, but the idea of it came to me in a dream one night. The fact that I had a birthmark that looked a bit scale-like cemented the design for me. I hated those ugly birthmarks, and they seemed to keep cropping up more often as I aged. This design disguised them perfectly. Even the tattoo artist thought it was pretty badass. Hurt like a motherfucker though.

I craned my neck in an effort to see the scales he was staring at, but it was useless. I wasn't as bendable as I was in my twenties. "I'm guessing there's probably like twenty-five by now?"

Eduardo shook his head. "That looks like a lot more than twenty-five. I'll have to count them one day," he said, leaning over to lick one, "with my tongue."

"You always were a stickler for actual data," I replied.

He slid off the bed then and tossed a sheet on me, so I wouldn't get cold. He was thoughtful, that one. "I'm gonna hit the shower."

"Mmm," I said, hugging the sheet around me. His cologne was intoxicating all on its own. Still, not a reason to keep a guy around. After this break, I'd need to be reassigned to a new team. Again. Maybe I'd try the London office. Lots more pasty-looking guys with bad teeth there. Less temptation.

"Hey, Tasha, get your ass in here with me!" Eduardo yelled over the noise of the rushing water.

"I'll be there in a minute." I grinned. No harm in enjoying him while I could. Though I needed to check in with work. I still hadn't gotten the official "you're clear for vacation" message, even though I put in for the time months ago. Sure, the work was easy, but the constant travel was weighing on me. I was looking forward to parking it in one place for the week.

Yanking the sheet off me, I yawned and walked, buck-naked, over to my phone. It was tucked into the back pocket of my pants.

As soon as I turned it on, notifications started pouring in, which was unusual. I didn't have friends or family—at least, none that knew this number—so I knew something big at work must have gone down overnight. Especially when all fifteen messages said the same thing.

**AGENT YOUNG, CALL THIS NUMBER ASAP.**

Purchase *The Lurkers Within* wherever books are sold.